"Hey! Who's been messing with my room?"

Rich had only closed his eyes for a minute—but when he opened them, nothing was the same. It was like waking up in a 1940s movie—only this was real.

Outside, he looked toward the towering oak, the one he'd passed a thousand times. It was gone. A struggling sapling stood in its place.

"I'm home all right—but something is terribly wrong!"

You'll also enjoy these other Pennypincher novels:

THE NEW KID, SPINNER, AND ME *Karen Sommer*

Satch and Spinner, 11, want to help a young Vietnamese boy named Hai feel at home in America. But when another friend takes an instant dislike to Hai, things get complicated.

SKY HOOK *Dan Jorgensen*

Out for basketball on the underdog junior high girls' team, Andrea discovers relationships, on and off the court, a bigger challenge.

SECRET OF THE PAINTED IDOL *Margaret Maddox Wallworth*

Suddenly Moshe, Kevin, and Sherry find themselves in 763 B.C. with the prophet Amos—confronting the fearful rites of the Baal worshipers! Sequel to *The Secret of the Silver Candlestick*.

A DREAM FOR DORRIE *Bonnie Sours Smith*

Dorrie, a high school senior, is torn. Does God expect her to become a missionary? Maybe. But Dorrie loves her hometown. And then there's David. . . . Sequel to *Dorrie and the Mystery of Angell Swamp* and *If You Love Me, Call Me Dorrie*.

BRAD BENSON AND THE SECRET WEAPON *Steve Swanson*

More than anything, Brad wants to be the star goalie of his school's hockey team. But the season is unexpectedly complicated by the arrival of the new Canadian player, Frenchy.

For a complete listing of all Pennypincher titles, write to Chariot Books, 850 N. Grove, Elgin, Illinois 60120.

The Year I Went to High School with My Parents

A Time Twist Adventure

Bill Bodell

Chariot Books
DAVID C. COOK PUBLISHING CO.

To Kathy, Bill Jr., Karen,
and the real Rich

Chariot Books is an imprint of David C. Cook Publishing Co.
David C. Cook Publishing Co., Elgin, Illinois 60120
David C. Cook Publishing Co., Weston, Ontario

THE YEAR I WENT TO HIGH SCHOOL
WITH MY PARENTS
© 1985 by Bill Bodell

Cover photo by Lance Clenard

First Printing, 1985
Printed in the United States of America
90 89 88 87 86 85   5 4 3 2 1

Library of Congress Cataloging in Publication Data
Bodell, Bill
  The year I went to high school with my parents.
  (A time twist adventure)
  Summary: Rich goes back in time to 1944, where he
meets his parents who are now his peers and finds them
very likable people.
  1. Children's stories, American. [1. Space and time—
Fiction. 2. Parent and child—Fiction]
I. Title. II. Series.
PZ7.B63516Ye 1985   [Fic]   85-9608
ISBN 0-89191-985-6

Contents

1
Rushing
Backwards

Ignoring the whine of enemy bullets, Rich Lawler pushed onward. He was halfway up the beach now, the landing craft far behind him.

Spit—spit—spit. The sound of machine gun fire.

In front of him, just to the left, came a series of explosions. The deadly line was headed directly at him.

Desperately, he lurched to his right.

Rich knew he was falling. His legs refused to move. His shoulder slammed against the hard surface.

"I've got to get up," he groaned. "There's a battle to be won."

The whining took on a metallic sound. Still dazed, Rich reached out, grasping for it. As he groped through the tangled mess, the ringing sound grew louder. At last Rich grabbed the offending object and spun over on his back. Sunlight blazed into his eyes, forcing them shut.

"Who is this?" The soft, accented voice seemed puzzled.

"What?" Rich struggled to clear his head. "Who are you?"

"Get up," the now-familiar voice commanded. "You can't lie there forever."

"Oh, yes I can." Rich shaded his eyes. "Give me a second." The lanky teenager forced himself awake. Lying on his bedroom floor, he could see his long legs tangled in the sheets.

The voice on the phone was Peko Asota's, an exchange student he'd befriended during the summer.

"Are you just getting up?" asked Peko.

"Yeah." Rich rubbed sleep from his eyes. "Watched TV until three o'clock."

"John Wayne movie, I'll bet."

"You're right. *Fighting Seabees*. 1944."

"Did we lose again?" His Japanese friend laughed.

"Sure did," Rich teased. "What's happening, man?"

"I'll meet you at Burger Crown in half an hour, okay?"

"Right," Rich said, hanging up the phone. Quickly he reached the bathroom across the hall and discarded the T-shirt and shapeless fatigues that served as pajamas. He tossed them toward the dressing chair as he stepped into the shower. Sliding the glass door shut, he watched the clothes slide off onto the air conditioning vent. As he soaped his hair, he made a note to pick up his sleepwear when he was finished.

Back in his room, Rich pulled his blue jeans over his shorts and took his socks from the top of the TV. Sliding into his worn track shoes, he searched the floor of the closet for his denim shirt.

Once dressed, he bounded down the carpeted stairs. His long strides took him directly to the refrigerator and a quart of orange juice. When the beverage neared the rim of his glass, Rich noticed the lightness of the waxed container.

He put his eye close to the opening. Only a fraction of an ounce remained. Finishing it off meant having to fold and dispose of the carton—either that or get bawled out. Rich pushed it to the back of the refrigerator, behind the iced tea.

His mother appeared from the pantry carrying a shopping bag.

"Why you wearing a sweater, Ma?"

"It's like the North Pole at the supermarket."

She placed a number of articles on the counter. "Besides, your father likes the house freezing when he comes home from playing golf."

Rich noted that all the items were things he'd put on the grocery list.

"You'd get pneumonia in the middle of a heat wave," he joked. For a moment he considered taking the supplies upstairs, but his watch told him it was time to leave.

"Where are you headed?"

"Meeting Peko downtown, then over to Julie's."

"Richard Lawler, friend of the friendless." His mother smiled and picked up the supplies. "You're a regular one-man welcoming committee." She placed the tubes and jars in his arms. "Where do you find all these strays?"

"They're not strays, Ma." With his chin, he nudged the slipping shampoo bottle back into place. "They're just new. They're neat when you get to know them."

Mrs. Lawler looked up at Rich. "Underneath that big macho image, you're just a softy."

Rich liked it when she told him that, but he wouldn't let it show. "Aw, Ma." He dashed up the steps with his loot and back down again, nearly slipping on a bar of soap he had dropped.

"Be home in time for supper, dear."

Rich knew he was running late. He thought for a moment of taking his bike, but decided he was too old for that at sixteen. *If only I had a car*, he thought. Ignoring the burning late summer sun, he stepped over the pushed-up section of sidewalk and sprinted down the long hill into town.

Peko sat patiently in a window booth. Rich waved and dashed inside. "Two Triple Universes, catsup only, large fries, and a super cola." Rich spread out the food. "Haven't eaten since yesterday," he told Peko.

"Air conditioning feels good."

Rich took a bite of the Triple Universe. "Aw, I could live without it." He turned to stare out at the traffic.

"Sure you could," Peko taunted. "Just like in the good old days." He snatched a fry. "You sound like your old man."

"Ah, so," Rich responded. "You're getting too Americanized. What happened to 'honorable father'?"

"You're watching too many old movies," said Peko. "You are confusing me with Charlie Chan."

After a second cola, Peko looked at his watch. "One thirty, I have to go."

"Me, too. Told Julie I'd stop by. Got to make you newcomers feel welcome."

When he got to Julie's, she was seated on the porch. "You look exhausted," Julie told him.

"And overstuffed." Rich rubbed his stomach.

11

"There's too much food in the world."

"Mom's in the backyard." Julie opened the door. "We can use the stereo in the family room."

"Any new tapes?"

"In my room," she said. "Want to look through them?"

"Julie?" a woman's voice called.

"What is it, Mother?"

"Is someone with you?"

"Rich Lawler. We're picking tapes to play downstairs."

"I'm finished in the garden. Play them in your room."

"Yes, Mother."

"Keep your door open."

Halfway through the first tape a louder call came up the stairs. "Close your door, Julie. That noise is driving me crazy."

Julie looked at Rich. They both laughed. "That's parents for you," she said.

Rich nodded in agreement. "I don't think they were ever young."

During the third tape, there was a knock on the door. Julie opened it to her mother, whose hands were over her ears. "Sorry, kids. Go for a walk or something before the house falls down."

"I'd better go," said Rich. "I'll call you when I get home."

At Ninth and Elm, where the Lawler's house

sat at the top of the hill, Rich debated going to the ice-cream stand.

"Richard!" his mother called. "You'd better come in and wash up for supper."

"Dad home already?"

"He will be soon."

Rich sauntered up the walk, his eyes checking the sky. He tripped on the section of sidewalk pushed up by the long tree root. He kicked it and then limped up the steps into the house.

"I wish that old tree were gone," said Rich. "And the sidewalk was fixed."

"It was fine when we moved in," his mother reminded him.

It seemed he'd hardly been on the phone a minute or so when he heard the sound of his father's voice.

"Rich, are you tying up that phone again?"

"Hold on, Julie. It's the old man." He covered the mouthpiece. "Be through in a minute," he yelled.

"Supper will be on the table in five minutes."

"Awright," Rich said impatiently. He went back to his conversation.

"Richard!" Dad's booming voice again. "Your food is getting cold."

Moments later, he was at the table transferring three large slices of roast beef to his plate. His eyes avoided the vegetables as he reached for a silver-coated baked potato.

"Ouch!" It dropped on his plate. "*That* sure wasn't cold."

"Gravy, son?" his father asked.

"Nuughh."

"Was that a yes or a no?"

"Now, dear," said his mother.

"What language are we speaking here?" asked his father.

"Have some vegetables, Richard," his mother added quickly. "They'll make you grow."

"I'm six foot two already, Ma." He put butter in the steaming potato. "I don't want to turn into a circus freak."

"When I was a boy . . ." his father began.

Rich had his father's favorite speech memorized by now.

"We were mighty glad to have vegetables to eat. But you young people. . . ."

Rich's mind drifted off to another world. He wondered what his parents were really like at his age. It was hard to believe they were as perfect as they claimed to have been. He swallowed the last piece of beef as the vegetable speech was ending.

"Did you listen to your father?"

"Yeah, Ma. What's for dessert?"

"Your favorite, rice pudding."

Six steps took him to the refrigerator and back. Three giant spoonfuls emptied the dish.

"Can I have another one?"

"Not now," said his father. "If you'd eaten your vegetables, you wouldn't still be hungry."

"I hate vegetables," Rich said wearily. "Can I be excused?"

"*May* I, dear," his mother answered. "It is *may* I."

Rich pushed back his chair.

"Sit and talk with us for a change," said his father. "What have you been doing with yourself?"

"Not much," he said. "Summer vacation's a real bore."

"You should have signed up for the church baseball team. They just won the county championship."

"Must be luck. Reverend Johnson doesn't know the first thing about baseball."

"It's obvious you haven't been to church in a while. Reverend Johnson retired two years ago."

"Oh," said Rich. The room was silent.

"You're excused, dear."

He dashed from the room, took the stairs two steps at a time, and bounded into his room. Julie's line was busy. Rich was embarrassed about not knowing there was a new minister at church. "Maybe I'll go some Sunday," he told himself. He dialed Peko's number. The buzz repeated in his ear.

Rich glanced around the room for something

to do. He pushed the air conditioning vent closed with his foot and looked up at the calendar hanging on his wall. He'd forgotten to tear off August. Day after tomorrow would be Labor Day.

Ripping the August page from his calendar, Rich crumpled it into a ball and tossed it toward his wastebasket. The wad of paper bounced off the rim and careened into the pile of litter surrounding the basket.

"No wonder I can't make the basketball team," he mumbled, turning back to the calendar on the flowered wall.

"Hey!" Rich gasped. "When did they paper my room with this awful stuff?"

He checked the date.

"There's something wrong with the calendar, too. It says September, and all thirty days are there." He looked closer.

Above the slogan "Buy War Bonds," in the inch-high letters indicating the year, Rich discovered the problem.

He blinked his eyes and looked again.

It still said . . . 1944.

2
A Mysterious Journey

A gust of wind exploded through the open window, flipping the calendar's pages wildly. Muffled music filled the room, scratching, throbbing. Strange but familiar. Near yet distant.

Cotton curtains surged into the room, riding the crest of the sudden storm. Snapping and cracking, they danced in rhythm to the scratchy tune.

Rich ducked instinctively, tripping over the phone. He fell backwards, landing heavily on the edge of the bed.

The wall calendar was gyrating now, held in place only by a stubborn nail. Up and over it spun, jousting with the swaying curtains, the raspy melody urging them on.

Dazed, Rich closed his eyes.

But only for a moment.

Slam! The window crashed down. His eyes jarred open.

Suddenly, the room was deathly still. It seemed different somehow—just like the music. Strange but familiar.

"Weird!" said Rich, rising from the neatly made bed. "Hey, who's been messing with my room?"

He looked toward his closet. A heavy curtain, suspended by a wooden pole, hung where the door should have been. Next to it, in place of his TV, was an old-fashioned radio.

Rich flipped on the knob. The radio lit up, then hummed, but nothing more. The tinny music persisted from across the room. He snapped the radio off and spun around to check his stereo. It, too, was gone. So were his endless stacks of tapes and records.

A dark red cabinet stood in the stereo's place. Five feet high, it had a domelike lid, a handle in the side, and two small doors in front.

Cautiously, Rich lifted the top. At once the scratching sound grew louder. He looked down. A heavy silver arm lay on a rapidly spinning record. The scratchy music offended his ears. Rich looked in vain for a plug to pull from the wall.

Squatting in front of the wooden cabinet, Rich yanked open the double doors. The music blared out, rocking him onto his heels. As he fell backwards, his head came to rest in a pile of argyle socks.

Covering his ears, Rich stared up at the blaring monster. Getting to his feet, he examined it closely. On the lid was a picture of a contented dog, a hollow cone by its side. Beneath it, the word "Victrola."

"Oh, no!" Rich shrieked. "They've destroyed our music."

Dashing out of the room, he skidded down the empty hall and down the noisy, uncarpeted stairs. Throwing open the screen door, he careened across the porch, nearly falling on the wooden steps.

Halfway down the sidewalk, Rich stared up at his open window. At last, the terrible music had stopped, replaced by an odd repeating sound. Kah-toosh, kah-toosh, kah-toosh.

"Not a bad beat," he grinned. "Could use some amplifiers, though."

Turning back to the street, he instinctively raised his foot to avoid the broken place in the sidewalk. He came down awkwardly, as if expecting a step that wasn't there.

"It's gone," he said, looking down at a straight line of cement. "But this is where the oak tree's root had pushed it up. When did Dad fix this?"

Rich looked toward the towering tree, the one he'd passed a thousand times. It, too, was gone. A struggling sapling stood in its place.

He checked the street sign. Elm. Then he looked back at the number on the porch. 901. He scratched his head. *I'm home all right—but something is terribly wrong!* Tingling fear crawled up his back as he crossed the street.

A clanking roar came from his left. While he watched, a steel-wheeled tractor bounced across the open ground, headed for a cornfield. Rich tried to get his directions straight. *A cornfield? This is supposed to be the Jackson's house.* Still puzzled, he headed down the hill toward town.

At Seventh, he crossed the red brick street. Its uneven surface resisted his shuffling gait. Where had the blacktop gone?

At Sixth, he stopped for a moment, running his fingers through his hair. The town was unusually quiet. Rich looked at his watch, then looked again. Hands and numerals had replaced the digital readout. He glanced back up Elm toward the top of the hill.

"Traffic should be coming in from the plant by now," he told himself. He surveyed the town and its endless line of roofs and chimneys. *Familiar,* he thought, *but something's missing.*

What is it?

An ancient car, but glistening and new, labored steadily up the hill. Its transmission growled.

"I'm walking through a late-night movie," Rich said aloud, "but it's in color and three dimensions."

At Fifth and Elm, he heard the giggling. Four teenagers stood at the corner watching him closely.

"Hello," said a boy. "Who are you?"

"Name's Rich." He felt his confidence returning. "I thought everyone in town knew that."

"Are you visiting here?" asked the taller girl.

"Me? I thought *you* were visiting here."

"Don't wise off to my sister," said the other boy, "or I'll bop you one."

"Bop me one?" Rich chuckled. "What's that mean?"

The shorter girl spoke up. "He'll smack you right in the snoot—that's what he means."

Rich didn't need any more confusion. "Cool it, man," he said with a smile. "I'm not looking for a rumble."

"Jeepers," the taller girl said. "You talk funny, that's for sure. We don't even have a car, never mind a rumble seat."

"Who said anything about a car?" Rich asked. He started to turn for home.

"Where do you live?" the first boy asked.

"Up there." Rich nodded. "901 Elm."

"Ninth and Elm!" the taller girl gasped. "Why, that's . . ."

The second boy's eyes opened wide. "The Krueger place?"

"Now wait a minute," said the first. "Ain't no kids at Old Man Krueger's."

"Sorry," Rich shrugged. "That's where I live."

"Then why do you look so poor?" the taller girl asked. "Mr. Krueger's a rich man."

"Poor? Who's poor?" said Rich. "My father's vice-president of Computer Technologies."

"Computer what?" the first boy asked. "Where's that supposed to be?"

"At Twenty-third and Elm," said Rich. "At the edge of town."

"Ain't no Twenty-third," said the second boy.

"Oh, yeah. Right on," Rich sneered. "No Twenty-third, and I'm a pauper. So what else is new?"

"Betty Jane didn't say you were a pauper," the first boy said. "Only that you *look* poor."

"That's right," said Betty Jane, the taller girl. "Who'd walk around in faded overalls if they could afford decent clothes?"

"And those ugly sneakers," said the other girl. "Ick!"

Rich looked down at his favorite outfit.

"Sneakers? These are joggers. Cost me thirty bucks." Putting his hand in his back pocket, he turned to show the label.

"That's different," said one of the boys. "He's got his name sewn on them."

"That's not *my* name," Rich explained. "These are designer jeans."

The teenagers howled in disbelief.

Rich was frustrated. He ran his fingers through his hair.

"Haven't you got a quarter for a haircut?" asked the other boy. "You trying to look like a girl?"

Rich opened his mouth to reply.

From across the street, a voice called out, "Ann Marie, you come right home. What have I told you about hanging around riffraff?"

"Coming, Mother," answered the shorter girl.

"What's riffraff?" asked Rich.

Ann Marie dropped her eyes. "I'm afraid you are," she said softly.

Rich saw the embarrassment in her eyes.

"Take it easy," said one of the boys.

"Sure," Rich answered.

"Toodle-oo," Betty Jane winked.

Rich watched them cross the street. Two pairs of baggy pants. Two billowing, flowery skirts. Four pairs of white socks and two-toned shoes. He scratched his head. *I've been watching too many late-night movies.*

Rich's mind was a jumble. First a calendar, then flowered wallpaper. The sudden storm, the old Victrola. A sapling where a tall oak should stand. His world was turning into an old-fashioned picture album.

Dazed, Rich wandered down another block. His reasoning rushed to keep up with his senses. He needed a reassuring symbol. At Fourth Street, he stared up at the steepled building. The familiar sign seemed a little fresher than he remembered it: Baxterville Community Church. Squinting, he made out the name below it: Rev. Jonathan Whitmer.

The sight of the church brought back his confidence. Logic was taking hold again. "Jonathan Whitmer," he said aloud. "That must be the new minister Dad told me about." Rich realized he hadn't been there in a while.

For a moment he considered going inside, then shook his head. He needed to be back in his room where he could think things through. Church was for kids and older people. He'd find his answers back in his room.

Rich was nearly back to Seventh before the truth began to register. The rooftops! Now he knew why they looked so strange. No TV antennas.

It really was 1944!

At the top of the hill, where the cornfield nestled into the corner of Ninth and Elm, Rich saw the tractor receding down the long dusty lane. The Elm Street pavement ended just past their property. On the horizon, a lonely farmhouse and barn were outlined against the summer sky.

That's all there was to Baxterville. No Twenty-third Street. No Computer Technologies. No . . .

"Welcome home, boy," said a voice.

Startled, Rich looked up toward the porch that should be his, but wasn't. A tall, gaunt, white-haired man stood at the top of the steps, his long thin fingers curled around the pillar.

Cautiously, Rich crossed the street and started up the walk.

"My name is Alvin Krueger," said the man, extending his hand. The warmth of his friendly greeting offset his rather imposing appearance.

"Hi," Rich gulped, "I'm . . ."

"Richard Alan Lawler the third," the old man smiled. "I've been expecting you."

"You have? But how . . . ?"

"Let me get you a lemonade. It's a very hot day."

"Okay," Rich nodded.

"Try the porch swing," said Mr. Krueger. "I'll be right back."

Rich stared at the big green object suspiciously. His eyes followed the stout links of chain from the solid wooden arms up to the spot where they met, then continued upward to the porch's ceiling.

Slowly he lowered himself into the suspended couch and pushed backward. The contraption creaked loudly. Rich's eyes darted to the hooks in the ceiling. They were holding tightly. The swing swung forward, then back again. By the time Mr. Krueger returned, Rich had it mastered. The creaking sound had become reassuring.

"Enjoying yourself, I see." The old man smiled. "Too bad your father took it down when he put in air conditioning. There's a lot of contentment in an old porch swing."

"Could be," said Rich. With one more push he swung out so far his long legs reached the railing. "Hey, I made it."

"When you're ready to land, your lemonade will be waiting." He put the tray on a nearby table. "No rush. This is a slower time you're living in now."

Rich slowed the swing. Hopping out, he reached for the frosty glass. Gulping it down, pain hit the roof of his mouth.

"Slowly," said Mr. Krueger. "It's a very hot day."

"Right," said Rich, as the sensation eased. Sipping more slowly, he thought as he pushed the swing back and forth.

"Mr. Krueger?"

"Yes?"

"How is it possible? How can I be here?"

26

"How can a cold drink feel as if it's burning the roof of your mouth?"

Rich stared at the glass. "Some things can't be explained, I guess."

"Precisely. . . . Now here comes an interesting couple," Mr. Krueger commented.

Rich looked at the approaching couple. "Big deal. More crummy teenagers."

Mr. Krueger laughed softly. "Look again."

The boy was tall and husky, much like Rich. He wore an open-collared sports shirt, beige slacks, and brown-and-white saddle shoes.

Rich turned his attention to the girl. She was petite and pretty, with long brunette hair down to her shoulders. She wore a white blouse, a light blue skirt, white anklets, and blue saddle shoes. She laughed gently, her hair swinging back and forth as she walked.

They turned left on Ninth and passed out of sight.

"That's gotta be the prettiest girl I've ever seen."

"In spite of her funny-looking clothes?'"

"Even that," Rich grinned. "Who are they?"

"Harley and Sue Ann. They pass by here frequently."

"Harley and Sue Ann! Gross!"

"No, their name isn't Gross." For a moment the old man looked puzzled. "They're about your age, though."

Rich scratched his head. "I'm not sure what my age is."

"For now, you're the same age as when you came. Sixteen."

"Will I ever go back?" Rich tried to hide his concern. "Back to the present?"

"For now, Richard, *this* is the present."

"Yeah," he said, pushing the swing. "The calendar, the changes in the town, the kids I met on the street. I guess part of it is sinking in."

"Think of the adventure!" said Mr. Krueger. "These are the good old days. You know, the days your parents have told you about over and over again."

Rich's eyes rolled upward at the thought. "I'll say."

Mr. Krueger's enthusiasm was growing. "What a rare opportunity you have! You'll be able to check it all out for yourself."

"That isn't really possible," Rich said. "People don't fly back and forth in time like that, do they?"

"Whatever you say, my boy." Mr. Krueger stood by the railing, holding up his glass. "I'm going for a refill. How about you?"

Inside, the second drink and the oscillating fan seemed to clear the remaining cobwebs from Rich's mind.

"Wait a minute," he said. "If this is the same town, except that it's 1944, then Mom and Dad

28

must be here."

"That's right."

"And they would be my age." Rich strained to remember. "Hey, this is the summer when they first met!"

"Sounds like you're beginning to enjoy your visit."

Rich leaned forward. "Tell me where to find them, Mr. Krueger."

"Oh, my, no. That would never do. What fun would there be in that?"

"You won't help me?"

"Not a bit." The old man's eyes twinkled. "Unless it becomes absolutely necessary."

"Then how do I explain myself?"

"We'll make you my grandson. Rename you Rich Krueger. Temporarily, of course. How does that sound?"

"Cool. I'd be like a secret agent from the future."

"And with your height, you'll be a perfect addition to our basketball team."

Rich cringed at the thought, remembering the missed shots that ringed his wastebasket.

"I couldn't slam dunk a shot if I stood on a ladder."

"What was that again?" Mr. Krueger asked.

"Nothing," said Rich. He felt more at ease knowing the old man didn't know everything about him.

"Any other questions, secret agent?"

"Won't my parents—the grown-up ones—won't they worry if I'm gone too long?"

"To them, the passage of time will be very brief."

"I wouldn't want them to think I ran off or anything."

"Very considerate of you, indeed. Now then, any other questions?"

"You mean I'll be going to school here? With my own parents?"

"That's right," said Mr. Krueger.

"And they won't know it?" Rich's eyes lit up. "Man, that's really weird."

"There are two things you must remember," Mr. Krueger added, leaning over the kitchen table. "A lot of what is history to you, hasn't happened yet in 1944. Don't forget that."

"I get it," Rich answered. "What's the second thing?"

The old man extended two bony fingers over his empty glass. "You can in no way let your parents—or anyone else—know who you really are."

"I promise," said Rich gravely. "I won't blow my cover."

"I'm sure that means something to you," said Mr. Krueger. "But I've no idea what you're talking about."

"Yeah, I see what you mean. I'll make sure to

learn the right words to use."

"They call it slang," sighed Mr. Krueger, "as meaningless to me as the things you say."

"How about 'twenty-three skiddoo.'"

"You've gone back forty years too far." The old man laughed. "Now go up and look around your room. It's all ready for you."

Rich climbed the once familiar stairs. At the end of the hall, he turned into the room which, in the natural order of things, was not yet his. Wearily, he lay down on the bed. He relived the strange day he'd been through, trying to sort everything out. His brain grew numb from thinking about it.

An hour later, Rich got up and went into the bathroom. Undressing, he stepped into the old-fashioned tub. He reached for the shower head. There wasn't any. He settled for a bath instead.

As the water rose up to his chest, he began to relax. Though he barely sensed it, Rich's hectic life was slowing down to a quieter pace.

Returning to his room, he opened the dresser and removed a pair of horrible striped pajamas. Rich looked in the mirror, then closed his eyes in dismay. The pajamas were a perfect fit—but, wow, did he look awful.

Rich turned on the radio, searching for a disc jockey's voice. He waited for the vacuum tubes to warm up. "Superheterodyne" it said on the radio. *Hah*, Rich thought, *there's nothing "su-*

per" about that.

At last he found the closing innings of a Detroit baseball game. From all he'd read, Rich knew it was a re-creation. In the background, the ticker tape clacked away. When it was over, the announcer, joyous over a late Tiger rally, confidently predicted the team would win the American League pennant.

"Save your energy, fella," Rich told the set. "The St. Louis Browns have this one all wrapped up!"

3
A Stranger in Town

Rich awoke to the knocking on his bedroom door, though he kept his eyelids tightly shut. Again came the knock, followed by the sound of the now familiar voice.

"Six thirty, Richard. Time to get up."

"Okay, Mr. Krueger. I'm awake."

"Breakfast will be on the table in a jiffy. Let's skedaddle."

Slowly, Rich opened one eye. The flowered wallpaper was still there. This was not a dream. Lying there, he wondered why he was so alert. Then he remembered turning off the radio the night before at ten fifteen.

Hopping out of bed, he searched for his T-shirt and jeans. They were gone.

"Gotta have something to wear," he muttered. "I'll try the closet."

Pushing back the curtain on the wooden rod, he stared into the closet in disbelief.

"Oh, no!" he wailed. "This is carrying things too far."

Rich searched through the neat array of pants, hooked to their hangers by inch-high cuffs. He took down a brown pair and tried them on. Immediately, his legs began to itch. Removing them, he read the label: 100% virgin wool.

"Not for me," he said, scratching his shin. "Maybe I'll chance the corduroys."

The shirts presented a difficult choice. All were hopelessly out of style; two-thirds of them checks or stripes, the remainder stiff white dress shirts.

Uncertain, Rich opened the door and called downstairs. "Where are we going today, Mr. Krueger?"

"Church, my boy. Did you forget it was Sunday?"

"Yeah . . . yes, sir, sort of, I guess."

"Hurry along, now. Your food is getting cold."

At the breakfast table, Rich rolled up the sleeves of his glistening white shirt, realizing how hungry he was. Soon the tall stack of pancakes was gone.

"Those were great, Mr. Krueger. Mom always fixes bacon and eggs."

"They're not easy to come by these days, what with a war on and all."

Rich wished he remembered his history as well as his baseball. "You mean food rationing?"

"That's right. Puts a damper on our menus, but we'll get by."

The old man drew a round watch from the little pocket below his belt. "Time to go," he said. "Need some help with that tie?"

"I guess so. Haven't worn one since confirmation class. Had to borrow one of Dad's clip-ons for that."

Mr. Krueger laughed. "So your father never did learn to tie a tie, eh? I'm not surprised. Glad to hear your folks had you confirmed, though."

"To be honest about it," Rich said, "I did it more to please them than anything else."

"Well, it's good to know you try to please your folks."

He began to replace the watch.

"Could I see that for a second?"

"Sure. Ever seen one like it before?"

"Dad used to have one. Called it his dollar watch. Is that really true? Does it really only cost a dollar?"

"That's all," said Mr. Krueger. "Check that tie in the mirror and see how it suits you."

"Hey, nice job. That's even better than one of Dad's."

"Slip on the jacket. Let's see how my mysterious new grandson looks."

Putting on his jacket, Rich thought of his role as a mysterious secret agent. "Neat," he said.

"Yes, you look very neat indeed."

"I meant about being a mystery man. I like the idea. Now we're both mysterious."

"Oh," said Mr. Krueger. "Are we?"

"That's what the kids I met yesterday said." Quickly, Rich changed the subject. "I'll bet you have a reason for taking me to church this morning."

"Certainly," he answered. "What better place to be on a Sunday?"

"How about in bed?"

"Or hunting or golfing?"

"I guess it's a matter of what a person considers important," Rich responded.

"You may be right," said Mr. Krueger.

When they arrived at the church, they sat near the front. Rich scanned the faces of the junior choir, wondering if his mother was among them. Two of the girls looked familiar; he remembered meeting them on the corner the day before.

Rich looked around the congregation, impressed by the large percentage of young people present. He wondered if there were as many in his family's church.

He looked again at the choir. The girl named Betty Jane looked back, curiously at first, and then smiled. He smiled back, wondering if his "old-fashioned" clothes had anything to do with her smile.

A nudge in the ribs from Mr. Krueger returned his attention to the service. The minister was talking about the wanderings of Jacob. Rich thought of his own journey; it was not one of distance, but rather, of time. He wondered how it would end.

After the service, he waited outside on the sidewalk as Mr. Krueger exchanged a few words with the minister. Rich was aware of being the object of some curiosity, especially among the young people.

In turn, he watched the passing faces carefully, hoping he might remember some from his mother's family album. One or two seemed vaguely familiar, or was it just his imagination?

"Hello," said the voice behind him. "You must be new in town, too."

Turning, he looked at a skinny boy in knickers and stifled the laugh inside him.

"Hi," Rich answered. "I'm sort of visiting my grandfather."

"Oh, who's that?"

Rich nodded toward the tall, gaunt man coming down the church steps.

"Mr. Krueger?" said the boy, his eyes opening wide. "I heard he's kind of spooky."

"Not when you know him," said Rich. He's a really nice guy."

"I'd better go. Here he comes."

"Hello there, lad," Mr. Krueger greeted the boy. Then he turned to Rich. "Aren't you going to introduce me to your friend?"

"I'd like to, Mr. Kr . . . Grandpa, but we just met."

"Dickie Branch, sir," said the high-pitched voice. "We moved here in July."

"A pleasure to meet you, young man. You must come up the hill and visit us sometime. Do you know where we live?"

Rich saw the young man tremble slightly before answering.

"Yes, sir. I expect nearly everyone knows where you live." Dickie looked around, as if searching for a familiar face. "I gotta go now. My mother's waiting." He dashed off down the street.

"How come he looks so scared?"

Mr. Krueger smiled. "I think it has something to do with old men who live alone in large white houses on top of hills."

"Beg pardon?"

"That's very fashionable in our young folks' reading these days."

"You mean that makes you mysterious?"

"Something like that."

"Are you?" asked Rich.

"What do you think?"

"I hadn't thought of it before. Now, I'm not sure."

They walked back up the hill in silence. On reaching the house, Rich picked up the Sunday paper from the porch steps. "PATTON RACES THROUGH FRANCE" read the headline.

"Interested in the war, lad?"

"In a way, I am," he replied. " 'Specially when I know how it's going to turn out."

"Do you like history in school?"

Rich made a face. "Naw, I think it's real boring."

"That headline certainly caught your eye."

"Yeah, but that's news."

"So is history," said Mr. Krueger, "except that it's condensed and written in books."

Rich thought about that for a moment. "But in history, I always know the ending."

"Always?"

"Well, maybe sometimes."

Silently, Rich read on. "Mr. Krueger," he said suddenly, "can you really go to a movie for thirty-five cents?"

"A quarter on Saturday afternoons."

"Wow."

Getting the sports section, he pored over its pages as though it were a hidden treasure. All the names that made him the baseball trivia master at school were laid out before him, complete with action photos.

He knew, of course, that most of the greatest stars were off to the service of their country; 1944 was not exactly baseball at its best.

He searched anxiously for the lineup of the St. Louis Browns, his sentimental favorite for that year. They were all there: Mike Kreevich, Vern Stephens, Chet Laabs, and the immortal Denny Galehouse, who was destined to become the team's first pitcher to win a World Series game. But where was Pete Gray, the one-armed out-fielder his dad had told him about?

Rich searched his trivia-laden mind.

"Nuts," he said. "That won't be until next year."

"Pardon me?"

"Sorry, Mr. Krueger, I was just talking to myself."

"You're quite a sports fan, aren't you?"

"Yes sir, 'specially baseball."

"What do you think of this young fellow with the Cardinals?"

"Who's that?"

"Musial. Stan Musial."

Rich thought before answering. "I think he looks very promising."

The old man howled with glee. "That was excellent. You'll do very well living in 1944."

"How long will I be here? Forever?"

"Oh, no, my boy. That wouldn't be possible if you really think about it. How could you be the same age as your parents?"

"I'd thought about that. There's no way one can change what has already happened. How long, then?"

"Long enough to suit your purpose."

For a moment Rich didn't respond. When he looked up, Mr. Krueger was staring at him.

"The answer to your question is 'yes.' "

"Yes?" asked the old man. "Yes to what?"

"The question you asked me earlier."

"Oh?"

"Yes!" Rich grinned. "You are mysterious."

Picking up his pipe, Mr. Krueger knocked the ashes from the bowl and smiled. "Good."

Just past three, after their midday meal, Rich pushed back his chair from the table. "I'm stuffed," he groaned.

"Cleaned your plate, I noticed."

"Everything was delicious, even the . . ."

"Yes?"

"Even the vegetables! I *never* eat vegetables."

"My, my," Mr. Krueger murmured.

"And you wouldn't have made a federal case of it if I hadn't?"

"Nope."

"Fact is, this is an unusual day. I hadn't been to church since I was confirmed."

"Hmm."

"And you wouldn't have bawled me out about it?"

"I hadn't planned on it."

"Well, I just thought . . ."

"You're a young man now, old enough to make up your own mind about what you want to do."

"I think I want to help with the dishes," Rich decided. "Then maybe I'll go for a walk."

As they worked in the kitchen, Rich's thoughts went back to the faces in the choir. "Was there anyone in that choir I should have recognized?"

"Did you recognize anyone?"

"I'd seen two of the girls yesterday. And the one with Harley Scott."

"Anyone that resembled your parents' old pictures?"

"They were in the class of '45. They gave up their yearbook because of the paper shortage. Crazy idea, I'd say."

"Oh, I hadn't heard about that."

"You confuse me at times, Mr. Krueger. I'm never sure what you know and what you don't know."

"Good. I'm beginning to like the idea of being a mysterious old man."

"One more question," added Rich. "Was my dad a member of this church? Was he there today?"

"Remember our bargain. That's for you to find out."

"That's the problem. For all the stories he tells, I've never heard the details of how they met, except that it was here in the summer of 1944."

"Oh?"

"I've looked through the family album from time to time. There aren't any pictures of him as a kid, either." Rich scratched his head. "What do you think of that?"

"Very mysterious," said Mr. Krueger.

4
First Day of School

The first day of school!

But hardly the way Rich had expected. He remembered the red brick two-story building as the village hall, in the center of town. But Central School was at the edge of town.

Rich passed the old cannon in the school yard, the one he remembered as brightly painted and sitting in the downstairs hall. His dad had told him it was the community's treasure. It had actually been fired in the French and Indian War. But now, the wooden wheels were slowly rotting. Black paint was peeling from the rusting barrel. A worn rope held it to the school's flagpole.

I guess it's not ready to become a treasure, Rich thought. He looked back at it over his shoulder. "I'm glad someone saved it," he said aloud.

Inside, he mounted the wide, creaking stairway to the second floor. Near the top, he stopped and glanced around. He could see into the room he knew as the mayor's office. But now a long table sat in the center of the room. On the table were Bunsen burners, test tubes, and all the appointments of a chemistry lab.

It reminded him of an old movie he'd seen. Any minute now, he imagined, Doctor Pasteur would come out proclaiming the existence of germs.

"Time's standing still," he exclaimed.

"Not on these stairs," said a voice behind him.

Rich turned around. Harley Scott was bounding up the steps two at a time.

"What?" asked Rich.

"Heard you say something about standing still." Harley grinned. "Try that at noon hour and you'll get trampled."

"Right," said Rich. "Never saw a school like this before."

"Something wrong with it?"

"Nope," answered Rich. "An old—a new school takes time to get used to."

"Where you headed?"

"Intermediate Algebra."

"Me, too," said Harley. "It's this way."

"I saw you go past the house the other day," said Rich, "with that pretty girl."

"You the new kid at Krueger's?"

Rich nodded.

"I've heard about you," said Harley.

"Good or bad?"

"Different." Harley laughed, "Come on, let's go."

By midafternoon they had become unwitting partners.

"You sure you didn't copy my schedule?" asked Harley.

"Positive," Rich said. He looked in his notebook. "Don't tell me you have World History next?"

Harley nodded. "Let's go. Looks like I can't get rid of you."

"I was thinking the same thing." Rich grinned.

When they entered the classroom, Harley nodded. "The back row. I need a nap."

"There's only one seat left."

"Don't worry. Someone will move."

As they approached, Dickie Branch, the timid boy Rich had seen at church, looked up. Gathering his books, he slipped out of his seat and moved up front.

"Told you so," said Harley. He sat down, placed his arm on the desk, and cradled his head in it. "Wake me up when it's over," he yawned, placing a book in front of his head.

The girl seated in front of Rich turned her head. The profile was vaguely familiar.

"You'll get in trouble, Harley," she said. "Here comes Mr. Davis."

She turned to face the front of the room. The teacher had closed the door and walked to his desk before it dawned on Rich who she was.

It was the girl he'd seen first with Harley, and then Sunday at church. Lou Ann Gross? No, that wasn't it.

"Welcome back, troops," said Mr. Davis. "The Allied forces are back on the continent, and Paris is free again!" He held up two fingers in a familiar gesture. "V for Victory."

The class applauded vigorously.

"The war will soon be over, boys and girls. We've got the Nazis on the run."

The enthusiasm surprised Rich. Somehow, he had the impression that it was America's fault whenever something went wrong in the world. "This sure is going to be an interesting class," he mumbled to himself.

Rich looked around the room. It didn't seem too different from the classrooms he knew. When Mr. Davis began discussing the Reconstruction period of the 1860s, Rich's mind began to wander. He found himself looking at hair. The girls all looked alike, except for the one with the ponytail. Fourteen boys, thirteen with short haircuts.

In the far row, over by the blackboard, sat the best-dressed kid in the room. His hair matched Rich's in length, his denim shirt and jeans were properly faded, and the rubber-soled shoes looked stylishly abused.

No peer pressure there, Rich thought admiringly. *He's his own man. Nice going, whoever you are.*

Suddenly, everyone was staring at him. The short-haired boys, the long-haired girls, even the ponytail. Last, but not least, Mr. Davis. Everyone but the slumbering Harley.

"Sorry to interrupt your thoughts, Mr. Krueger."

Rich looked around the room.

"You are Richard Krueger, aren't you?"

"Yeah," he mumbled, the new name locking into place. "That's me."

Mr. Davis stared at him sternly. "I beg your pardon."

"I mean, yes, sir, I'm Richard Krueger, all right."

The teacher's face softened. "It's your first day. I won't take you to task too severely."

"Thanks," said a relieved Rich.

"Now to my question, Richard. When did the

last war end?"

Rich was eager to redeem himself. "1973," he blurted.

The howls of laughter woke the dozing Harley from his nap.

"Very funny, Richard," said the teacher. He turned to Harley. "Would you like to try that one, oh, slumbering giant?"

"1918," answered the bleary-eyed Harley.

"Thank you," said Mr. Davis. "Now return to your rest."

Again the classroom howled. *This guy knows how to control a class,* Rich thought.

Leaving class he was still embarrassed, with no one to blame but himself. He was supposed to be the witty one. People were supposed to laugh *with* him, not *at* him.

Reaching his locker, Rich pulled the combination to the lock from his pocket. After dialing, he pulled sharply on the door. It flew open, hitting a girl near the next locker.

"Hey!" she screamed. The books in her arms tumbled to the floor.

"Watch it, stupid," Rich growled.

She stooped down to retrieve her scattered papers. "You're certainly ill-mannered."

"I'm cool, man," he answered.

The girl tossed her long hair. "You don't see well either. I'd have sworn I was a girl."

The gathering students laughed. Rich wasn't

used to that.

"Help her pick up the books, jerk," said a boy.

Reluctantly, he bent over and scooped up a geography book. "Sue Ann, that's it," he said, reading from the cover.

She continued to ignore him, not bothering to look up.

Awkwardly, Rich retrieved two pencils and placed them in the top of her locker. Head down, he broke through the circle of students and headed for the stairs.

Why did he let her intimidate him like that? Why did the unsmiling eyes of his fellow students bother him? Rich shook his head and promptly bumped into someone else.

"Hey, watch it!" yelled Harley, a stack of books under his arm.

"It's my day for clumsiness," apologized Rich.

"Accentuate the positive," Harley replied. He tucked the books into the crook of his arm. "Nobody takes me off my feet. Not even you."

"I messed up again. Not a very impressive start."

"You've had a rough day. How about a spin?"

"A spin?"

"Sure." Harley pushed open the front door. "My car's right here."

Rich stared at the shiny relic. "Neat. A '39 Ford?"

"You're close," said Harley. "It's a 1940. With

50

a rumble seat, too." He winked knowingly.

"I've heard about them. Let's see how it works."

"No fooling? Never seen a rumble seat?"

"Not up close," Rich added hastily.

Harley put his books through the open window. At the rear of the car, he inserted a key in the lock just under the back window. Turning it, he pulled on the handle. The section swung open, revealing another seat.

"Hey!" said Rich. "It's like opening a trunk, only upside down."

Harley stared at him momentarily. "I suppose you could put it that way."

"Fantastic! People can really sit in there."

"That's for sure," said a puzzled Harley. "What did you expect?"

"Terrific for sneaking into a drive-in."

"Who'd want to sneak into a drive-in? You mean like a custard stand?"

Rich remembered his dad saying there were no drive-in movies in Baxterville till after the war. "Ah, no. I was thinking of a milk shake or something."

"That's different," said Harley. "Hop in." He closed the rumble seat and slid behind the wheel.

"Good to be in a car again," Rich commented. "Let's go."

Harley roared out of the school yard, a cloud

of dust in his wake. Pulling onto the side street, he coasted through a stop sign and headed out of town.

"No cop, no stop," said Rich.

"That's keen," laughed Harley. "Never heard that one before."

"I've got a million of 'em," Rich answered. He'd heard that one in an old Jimmy Durante movie.

Harley smiled knowingly. "Goodnight, Mrs. Calabash, wherever you are."

Rich was breaking through the language barrier. He felt at ease for the first time all day. As he cranked down the window, he noticed the black stamp on the windshield. "What's the A stand for?" he asked.

"Nonessential driving," explained Harley. "You don't know about that?"

"Oh, sure," said Rich. He remembered his dad talking about gasoline rationing during the war. "But I don't have a car."

"Yes, sir," said Harley. "I'm as nonessential as you can get according to the government."

"How much gas does an A stamp allow?"

"Four gallons a week."

Rich thought about that. "You sure you can afford to be doing this?"

"Afford it? It's less than a buck's worth."

"I mean the four gallons. Won't you run out, driving around like this?"

"My old man's a farmer," Harley answered. "Gets all he needs. Who's to say where he chooses to use it?"

"I see," said Rich. "At least, I think I do."

"Everyone walks, even most of the teachers. I'm the only kid in school with a car."

"That must make you pretty popular."

"You bet," grinned Harley.

Two miles out of town, they turned right onto a dirt road. A sagging house, its unpainted wood turning black, appeared on their left.

"Welcome to Poverty Ridge."

"This is your place?" gasped Rich.

"Loren Hopkins lives here," said Harley. "Folks used to have a big farm. Lost everything during the depression."

"Loren Hopkins. Do I know him?"

"The long-haired guy. He's in our history class."

"With the faded jeans and denim jacket?"

"I feel sorry for him," Harley said. "Can't afford decent clothes or shoes. Can't even afford a haircut."

"I thought he looked fine."

Harley stepped on the gas. "You're kind of strange." He reached into the glove compartment and withdrew a box, offering it to Rich. "These are hard to get. Want a drag?"

Rich shook his head. "I'm not into pot."

"Pot? What's pot?"

"Marijuana. It's plain stupid."

"Krueger, I wonder about you. Don't you know a cigarette when you see one?"

"You'll end up with cancer."

"You're worse than my old lady. She says it'll stunt my growth."

Rich grinned, "You're over six feet, aren't you?"

"Six two."

"Maybe you'd have been seven feet tall without them."

"Yeah, I might even make all-conference center."

Harley turned left at the next crossroads, leaving Poverty Ridge behind in a cloud of dust. He pointed to the large white house ahead with its red farm buildings and towering silo.

"That's our place." He slowed at the driveway. "Come on in for a few minutes."

Rich felt he couldn't have picked a better friend. "Sure," he said, "I'm enjoying the freedom."

"You must feel like a prisoner with your grandfather."

"Sometimes." Rich thought of the big house set on the hill and set back in time. "It's not what I'm used to."

Harley passed the house and drove down the lane. Parking at the corncrib, he pointed to a tall, thin pump. A round glass bowl with a flying red horse etched on its face sat on top.

"There's our gas rationing." He laughed. "Bring old man Krueger out sometime. We'll give him a fill-up."

Rich felt uneasy. "He probably wouldn't take it."

Harley got out of the car. "I suppose not," he said.

Rich felt he was being watched. Turning, he saw a tall woman waiting on the porch.

5
Dangerous
Games

"That's my ma," said Harley. "You'd better be hungry."

"Too early for supper." Rich's stomach grumbled.

"We don't eat supper till dark, after the chores are done."

"You work around the farm?" Rich hadn't expected that.

"Thirty-five cents an hour," Harley said proudly.

"Thirty-five cents!"

"More than most kids around here get. Old

man's pretty generous."

Inside, Mrs. Scott took a big selection of foods from the double-doored refrigerator.

"Wow!" Rich stared at the table. "Haven't seen so much food since I got here."

"That's one of the advantages of living on a farm," said Mrs. Scott. "Harley is a big eater."

"So was I, once." Rich remembered the bowl of cereal for breakfast and the jelly sandwich and glass of milk that made up his lunch. His mouth began to water.

"Dig in," said Harley.

"This must be a whole week's ration stamps, Mrs. Scott." Rich had examined the coupons in Mr. Krueger's ration book, with the different colors determining how much of the scarce food items a person could buy.

There was a strange, troubled look on Harley's face as he looked up at his mother.

"Did I say something wrong?" Rich asked.

"Dig in, boys." Mrs. Scott laughed and winked at her son. "We watch our stamps carefully, don't we, Harley?"

Harley hesitated and then spoke quietly.

"That's right, Ma."

They piled the food onto their plates and then ate in silence. Mrs. Scott busied herself at the sink, occasionally looking up and down the road.

A long gray car pulled slowly into the driveway. The driver got out. Mrs. Scott went out through the screen door and met the man in the yard. Together, they walked back to the cellar doors.

Five minutes later, they reappeared. Each of them carried two large brown bags over to the car and put them in the trunk. After closing it, the man reached into his wallet and removed several bills. Mrs. Scott slipped them into her apron pocket as the car turned and drove off.

"Looks like you've got a good business going out here."

Harley eyed Rich suspiciously. "What do you mean by that?"

"Hey," he replied. "I didn't mean anything by that."

"Sure," said Harley, his face sullen. "Finish up and I'll show you around."

They walked past the farm buildings and part way down the lane. On the way back, Rich belched loudly. "That's the biggest meal I've had in a long time," he apologized.

Harley grinned, his attitude seeming to soften. "We've got a big place," he said, indicating the farm's vast expanse. "Sure beats the ration books."

"What happens to all the extra you produce?"

A steely look came over Harley's face. "That's for us to know and you to find out."

Rich realized he had struck another sensitive area. He changed the subject quickly. "That's a nice barn."

"I'll show it to you."

"I should be getting back."

"Come on," invited Harley. "Just a few minutes."

Sliding open the barn doors, they climbed to the empty hayloft above.

Rich stood in the center of the cavernous room, the peak of the roof two stories above him.

"Stop right there," the retreating Harley commanded. "And don't turn around."

Behind him, Rich heard a thunking sound. Before he could turn in its direction, a large orange sphere flew past his head. He watched it arch downward and smack through the middle of a bushel basket nailed to the opposite wall.

"Yahoo!" yelled Harley. "How's that for a shot?"

"Fantastic," said Rich. "Can you do that in the gym?"

"Almost," Harley admitted. "Could do better if Coach would let me bring my own baskets."

"You need a backboard. You could have banked it in."

"Tell my old man that. He won't let me put one up." Harley retrieved the bouncing ball.

"I'm surprised. I thought you got everything you wanted."

"Oh, sure," said Harley. "As if I want this sore

back from pitching hay into this loft—or baling straw or building fences."

"Don't be so defensive. It doesn't seem to have hurt you any."

"You sound like my old man. Builds muscles, he says."

Suddenly, he shot the ball to Rich, who let it bounce off his arms. As Harley dashed after it, Rich tripped. Grabbing the ball, Harley made another basket.

"You're pretty clumsy, Rich."

"Basketball was never my game."

"Too bad. We need help on the varsity this year." Harley handed him the ball. "Want to try some free throws?"

At the imaginary line, Rich balanced the ball in one hand, the way he'd seen the pros do it on TV. He pushed the ball off in a high arc. It came down a foot short of the basket.

"Where did you learn to shoot like that?"

"That's how everyone does it."

Harley shook his head. "No one I've ever seen. Here, let me show you the right way."

Holding the ball in both hands at his waist, Harley bent his knees. Lifting the ball up in a gentle curve, he plopped it in through the center of the basket.

"You've got a lot to learn, Rich. We're going to need your height this winter."

Rich didn't answer. He dashed after the ball

instead, saying, "Show me how you did that again."

As time passed, Rich got the feel of the ball. The primitive surroundings intrigued him. "Do you come up here a lot, Harley?"

"Sure. Every chance I get."

"Just to practice basketball?"

Harley hesitated. "That and other things. It's a good place for thinking things out." Just as quickly as it came, his thoughtful mood was gone. "You're a lousy basketball player, you know."

"It's too dark to see anything," Rich protested.

"If I brought in a dozen lights, you still couldn't hit that basket."

"You're right," Rich grinned. The smile froze on his face. "Oh, no! I'm in big trouble."

"What's wrong?"

"If it's dark, I've missed supper!"

"You're hungry again?"

"Not that. I never told Mr. Kr . . . Grandpa where I was."

The boys scrambled down the ladder and across the barn floor. As they slid the big doors shut, all the yard lights went out.

"What happened?" Rich asked.

"Nothing to worry about," said Harley, but his voice sounded worried. "It's this way to the car. I'll drive you home."

Harley had just slipped behind the wheel when the glare of headlights blazed through their windshield. Rich could barely make out a big truck easing itself down the drive.

Suddenly, the truck came to a stop, its brakes squealing in the still night air. Then the truck turned to its right, toward the silo. Gears growled and clunked as it shifted into reverse.

"What's going on?" Rich asked,

"Be quiet," Harley whispered.

The truck edged backward toward the house, stopping just short of the cellar stairs. Rich saw the dim figure of a man get down from the cab and make his way toward the back.

Something clanged. A steadily widening sliver of light illuminated the rear of the vehicle. Rich realized the cellar door was opening.

"What do we do now?" Rich asked. It was getting late.

"Nothing," Harley said. "We sit and wait."

"But I've got to get home. Can't you pull around him?"

Harley's voice was soft but insistent. "We'll sit and wait."

Rich peered out into the darkness. A man emerged from the cellar stairs. Two men from the truck stood talking to him. Then all three disappeared below.

One by one, the three emerged carrying large boxes. They lifted them up to waiting hands inside the truck. Back and forth they went, till it seemed the vehicle could hold nothing more.

Finally, the truck doors clanged shut. Two men faced each other at the top of the stairs. At last, one returned to the truck. The other went down the cellar steps, pulling the heavy doors closed behind him.

The night was pitch black.

The heavy engine turned over and started. Slowly, the truck growled up the lane and onto the road. When the headlights went on and the truck shifted into second gear, it was already one hundred yards up the road.

When it was out of sight, Harley started the car. He turned on the lights, headed up the lane and turned the opposite direction into town.

"I don't think I should ask what that was all about," Rich said.

"A good decision," Harley agreed. He seemed determined to keep his voice steady.

They passed through town and up the hill, only the sound of the balloon tires on the brick street breaking the silence.

At Ninth Street, Harley pulled to the curb.

"Tell your grandpa it's my fault you're late."

Rich opened the door. "My fault as much as yours."

"Hold it," said Harley, reaching behind him. "Here's two cartons of eggs. Ma put them in the car for you."

"Thanks," said Rich. "I'll be sure not to drop them."

Harley forced a smile. "That's a month's worth of ration stamps, you know."

"I enjoyed myself," Rich said. "And thank your mother, too."

Harley made a U-turn in the intersection, heading the car back down the hill. Clutching his precious cargo, Rich decided not to run up the sidewalk. Being a few seconds later wouldn't make that much difference.

The house was strangely quiet. He put the eggs in the refrigerator and then peeked into the living room. Mr. Krueger was dozing in his chair. The evening paper had slipped from his lap. Rich tiptoed across the room, headed for the stairs.

"Richard?"

"Yes, Grandpa?"

Mr. Krueger pulled out his watch and studied it closely. "You're rather late getting home, aren't you?"

"I'm sorry. I know I should have called."

"Your apology is tentatively accepted," the old man grumped. "I'll decide for sure after I've heard the details."

Rich sank into the couch. "It seems as if this day has been forever." A feeling of tiredness came over him, far different from last week's boredom. When Rich told of the incident in history class, the old man smiled.

"I should have realized Mr. Davis was referring to the First World War. I wasn't thinking."

As he related the incident at his hallway locker, the smile disappeared from Mr. Krueger's face.

"That doesn't sound very gentlemanly to me," he said.

"I felt dumb about it afterward." Rich fiddled with the pillow on the couch beside him. "I thought I was being funny, but nobody laughed."

"Including the girl?"

"Her? She gave me a good bawling out. It reminded me of . . ." His voice trailed away.

"Yes?"

"I know this sounds stupid . . . but it was kind of like when my mom . . ." Suddenly Rich's eyes opened wide. "Grandpa, is it possible that . . ."

Rich felt as if he were working a crossword puzzle.

"No, it couldn't be," he said. "It was the girl who went by here with Harley Scott. Besides, her name is Sue Ann something. My mother's name is Susan."

"Oh?"

"And she acted pretty haughty. Didn't even notice me."

"Was that a blow to your ego?"

Rich thought for a moment. "Naw, she's too

interested in Harley. She's awful pretty, though."

"Poor Rich."

"The more I think of it . . . Mr. Krueger, could *she* be my mother?"

"What makes you think that?"

"It's just a feeling. The way she talks; the way she looks. When she bawled me out at that locker, it gave me a spooky feeling." Rich got up and paced the floor. "Yep. It has to be my mom." He turned to look at Mr. Krueger. "Am I right, Grandpa?"

The old man nodded. "You're halfway home. That was your mother all right."

"But the name. Sue Ann? Her name is Susan, not Sue Ann."

Mr. Krueger chuckled, "Then your mother has a secret I didn't know about. You see, back here in the '40s, it's very common for young ladies to have two names. Sue Ann, Mary Lou, Betty Jane—an endless string of them, it seems."

"It's been in the back of my mind all day, only Harley and I . . ."

"So you spent some time with Harley Scott?"

Rich nodded. "Since after school until just now." He recounted his day up to the basketball game in the hayloft.

"And what's your opinion of young Mr. Scott?"

"In one way, he's a lot of fun. He's got his own car, the kids seem to like him, and he always has money to spend."

"And in the other way?"

"It's hard to explain. In this time and place, when everyone else is sacrificing and doing without—well, I guess he seems like a spoiled brat."

"That's quite an admission."

"And I don't like him for liking my mom."

"I understand the attraction is all one way. Harley would like her to be serious about him, but she really isn't."

Rich looked relieved. "I'm glad to hear that. Otherwise things wouldn't have added up."

"No." Mr. Krueger smiled. "Your mother didn't fall in love with Harley."

"Then where does my dad come into the picture?"

"Ah, that's for me to know and you to find out."

"That's the second time I've heard that one today. Harley said it this evening."

"Then there's more to the story with Harley?"

"Yeah, the most disturbing part, actually." Rich went on to tell him about the truck that came after dark and of Harley's discomfort.

"Did your history books tell about the black market?"

Again, Rich wished he had studied more. "It

had to do with rationing and crooks, didn't it?"

"With the war going on, our citizens are doing without a great many things to make sure our soldiers have enough. Scarce items are rationed, with everyone getting only what they need."

Rich thought of the big supper he'd had at Harley's. "Most people, that is."

"There's always someone who'll take advantage," Mr. Krueger sighed. "They'll profit at any price, even if it means breaking the law."

"Like Prohibition in the '20s and '30s?"

"That's one example."

"And that's what Harley's father is doing?" Rich asked. "He's a black marketeer?"

Mr. Krueger nodded. "He takes in goods intended for law-abiding people and sells them off to the highest bidder."

"Then why isn't he in jail?"

"A good question, my boy. Why isn't he?"

"In my time, we call that ripping off the system. Lots of people think there's nothing wrong with it."

"Some things never change," said Mr. Krueger. "It makes things bad for Harley."

"I remember a line from when we studied *The Merchant of Venice*. 'The sins of the fathers are to be laid upon the children.' It doesn't seem fair."

"It isn't," Mr. Krueger agreed. "The Bible says, 'Come to me, all who labor and are heavy laden, and I will give you rest.' "

"And that applies to Harley?"

"Yes," said Mr. Krueger. "When Harley's burdens get heavy enough, perhaps he'll turn to God."

"He doesn't belong to our church, does he?"

"He did, though I haven't seen him there in recent years. Some young people don't think going to church is fashionable anymore."

Rich looked away.

Mr. Krueger continued, "You've had a long day, young man. You'd better be off to bed."

"I haven't told you about the eggs."

"The eggs?"

"Harley's mother sent home two dozen eggs for us," said Rich. "I don't think I want to eat them now."

"Nor do I."

"I'd feel guilty eating them, but I'd feel guilty throwing them away."

"So what do you suggest?"

Rich thought for a while. "Could we give them to someone?"

"There's the USO here in town. People volunteer their time to feed and entertain the soldiers from Fort Arnold," Mr. Krueger said. "Perhaps they could use the eggs."

"I could stop there after school tomorrow and drop off the eggs," said Rich. "Maybe our servicemen would enjoy a nice, fresh omelet!"

6
An Impossible Choice

Rich saw a lot of Harley Scott in himself. As the days passed, he wondered if he liked what he saw.

"He's a BMOC," said Steve Kristl, a new friend from English class.

"You've got me there," Rich admitted. "We don't use that expression where I come from."

"Big man on campus."

"Oh, I knew that," Rich said, recovering quickly. "I wouldn't call that field next to the school a campus, would you?"

"Guess you're right," grinned Steve. "Hadn't

thought about it that way."

"More like a big fish in a little pond."

"I like that," said Steve. "Wish I had the nerve to call him that. Wait till I tell the other guys."

Inside, Rich was pleased with himself. Once again one of his father's outdated expressions had come in handy. It was slowly dawning on him that the old man might have been pretty sharp in his day.

"It's taken me a few weeks to get adjusted," said Rich. "This school is like being in a whole different world."

Steve got up from the bench where they'd been sitting. "You've fit in pretty well so far," he said. "Though some of us wondered when we saw you speed out of here with Harley that first day."

"How about that Branch kid? He's new, too. How's he doing?"

"He's a strange one," said Steve. "Keeps to himself pretty much."

"I guess he doesn't have my winning personality."

Steve looked at him, grinning. "Or your basic humility, either."

The school bell signaled the end of the lunch period.

"Have you heard about the yearbook?" asked Steve.

"About not having one this year?"

"What do you think they'll decide?"

Rich got up from the bench. "I hadn't really thought about it much." They started up the sidewalk toward the school. "Do you think it would really help anything?"

"Harley is all for scrapping it. He's pretty patriotic when it comes to the war effort, you know."

Rich thought back to the big truck of black market food he'd seen and the gas Harley used for his daily joyrides. "He certainly talks that way, doesn't he?"

They reached the school door.

"I think you're beginning to see through Harley," observed Steve, opening the door. "He blusters a lot."

"I can't for the life of me figure what Sue Ann sees in him." The words were out before Rich could stop himself.

"So that's it," said Steve. "Sounds like you're kind of interested in her yourself."

"Not the way you think," Rich stammered. "She seems too nice a girl for a blowhard like that."

"She is a nice girl," Steve agreed. "Won't even let Harley drive her home."

"I don't blame her. Harley calls that car his girl trap."

They climbed the stairs together and crossed

the hall to the English room.

"Let's go," said Steve. "Today we'll find out if we have to get our pictures taken."

"Pictures?"

"For the yearbook."

Following Steve into the room, Rich thought about yearbooks. He knew his parents' class gave up its yearbook to help the war effort and the paper shortage in 1945. He tried vainly to remember if his parents' pictures were in the 1944 yearbook—or if there even was one in 1944! As Rich slipped into his seat, waiting for the class to begin, he knew no more than his fellow students.

It was clear that Mrs. Nelson, their teacher, was in a dilemma. "I know you are interested in how the senior class voted on the yearbook," she said.

The class waited, expectantly.

"The vote was 14 to 14," Mrs. Nelson announced. "They voted three times."

"Bunch of Nazi lovers!" said Harley.

"Enough of that, young man," snapped Mrs. Nelson.

"What happens now?" asked Betty Jane.

"The seniors wanted me to vote to break the tie," Mrs. Nelson went on. "I offered them another alternative, which they accepted."

"What's the alternative?" someone asked.

"I told them that, unless the war ended, the

junior class would be faced with the same question next year." The teacher walked from behind her desk to the front row of the class. "I suggested they might let you break the tie."

"And they agreed to that?" asked Sue Ann. "We lowly juniors get to decide?"

"Frankly," said Mrs. Nelson, "if it were up to me, I would have voted not to have one." Turning, she walked to the blackboard and drew a large *T* in the center.

Ann Marie raised her hand.

"Yes?" asked the teacher.

"So no matter which side you had been on, there would have been fourteen votes against your decision."

"Our class philosopher," said Harley in a loud whisper.

"That's correct, Ann Marie. Now, if you want the responsibility, the decision is up to all of you."

"Let's make it unanimous to cancel the yearbook," said Harley.

"Let's have some discussion first," Steve responded. "This is still a democracy, isn't it?"

The teacher nodded at Harley. "All right, Harley, we'll begin with you."

The tall boy strode to the blackboard. Above the left side of the *T* he wrote *Americans;* above the right side he wrote *Axis Powers.*

"It's as simple as that," he said. "Vote to

donate the paper to the war drive." He placed a big X on the left side of the board. "But if you're a friend of Hitler and Tojo and Mussolini, then put your mark on the right with the traitors!"

Triumphant, Harley returned to his seat to the cheers of several classmates.

"It's not as simple as that," said Ann Marie.

Many of the boys, led by Harley, began to hoot.

"Let her talk," interrupted Steve. He turned to face Harley. "You're sounding like Hitler yourself."

The sharp crack of a ruler on Mrs. Nelson's desk quickly brought order. "If you're going to continue to act like this," she said, "I'd do better going downstairs and asking the first graders. Go ahead, Ann Marie."

The girl looked at the glowering Harley. "It's all right," she said in a soft voice. "That's all I wanted to say."

The room grew still.

Mrs. Nelson looked about. "Is that the end of the discussion then?"

A hand in the front went up.

"Yes, Dickie?" she said. "What do you have to say?"

"He shouldn't even be allowed to talk," said Harley. "What does he know about this school?"

Slowly, the slim youngster rose to his feet. "I don't know much about this school, that's true, but I do know as much as anyone else about why we're fighting this war."

"Tell us all about it," Harley sneered.

"I thought the whole purpose was to give conquered people in Europe and elsewhere a chance to regain their freedom; to give them a chance to express their opinions without fear of retribution." He looked at Ann Marie. She smiled back at him.

"I don't know whether our decision on the yearbook will make a difference in the winning or losing of the war," Dickie continued. "What's important to us in this room will be the manner in which we decide it."

"He's right," said Betty Jane.

"Let's make it a secret ballot," Steve added.

"Hooray for Dickie Branch," said another student. "It's about time someone stood up for the average person."

Mrs. Nelson waited for other comments. When none came, she returned to her desk and began cutting up slips of paper. "Are we agreed then on a secret ballot?"

The majority of the heads nodded.

Rich had been holding his counsel, mindful of the warning given him by Mr. Krueger: "You cannot do anything that will in any way change the future."

He stared long and hard at the ballot before him. He knew the printing of a small yearbook in an obscure town would not really change the course of the war. But he had, or was cursed with, the advantage of hindsight. *Things seem so simple when you look back*, he thought.

Mrs. Nelson was starting down the far aisle, collecting the slips. He had to decide quickly.

Curling his left hand around the ballot, he moved his pencil over the paper. Then he folded the sheet and held it out for the approaching teacher.

One by one, Mrs. Nelson opened the slips and put them on her desk. Halfway through, she hesitated, looked at both sides of the ballot and placed it in the center.

She completed her count and sighed deeply.

"The vote is thirteen to twelve," she announced, "in favor of having a class yearbook."

"Hey, wait a minute," said Harley. "There are twenty-six in this class. Thirteen and twelve is only twenty-five."

"You get an *A* in arithmetic," mocked Ann Marie.

Mrs. Nelson held up one slip. "One person didn't vote," she said. "Of course, that's an individual's right, too. I'll admit I'm disappointed in how the vote turned out." She sighed deeply, "But it won't be the first time or the last."

She walked to the door of the classroom. "Sue Ann, will you take over for me? I must let the seniors know the results."

All through history, which ended the school day, it was obvious that Harley was still very angry. At the final bell, he stormed out of class and down the hall.

Alone in the classroom, Rich thought through what he had done earlier in the afternoon. If he had marked his ballot in favor of canceling the yearbook, he would have created a tie vote. With Mrs. Nelson having already expressed her opposition to it, the yearbook would never have been printed.

If he had voted in favor of the yearbook, his vote would simply have increased the margin of victory. On reflection, he realized his decision not to vote was the proper one. He had not changed the course of events in any way.

Sitting there, Rich resolved one thing: when he returned to his own time he would begin a vigorous search for the controversial 1944 yearbook.

Walking down the hall, he noticed the cluster of students near the lockers. To his surprise, Dickie Branch was in the center of the group.

"It's about time someone stood up to Harley Scott," said Steve Kristl. "You've got more guts than sense."

"You were positively heroic," Ann Marie added.

"I think Harley sees too many war movies,"

Dickie said. "He thinks it's all glamorous."

"We saw him at the theater Saturday night," said Betty Jane. "That John Wayne movie about construction battalions in the South Pacific."

Fighting Seabees," said Rich.

"That's the one," said Steve. "Were you there?"

Rich hesitated. "I saw it before."

"Maybe the Seabees could use some of that gas he burns up every day with his joyrides," said Sue Ann.

"He's some superpatriot," agreed Steve.

Rich closed his locker and watched Steve, Ann Marie, and Betty Jane continue down the hall.

"You were very courageous," said Sue Ann quietly.

"Thanks," Dickie answered. He turned to Rich. "Are you leaving now?"

"Not yet," said Rich. "I'll see you later."

Rich went back to the English room for a book he had left behind. Pausing, he looked at the blackboard where Mrs. Nelson had drawn the *T*; he thought once more of his decision on the class balloting.

Maybe Mr. Krueger had something when he said history was news in a condensed form. Rich thought of his father, who collected history books as avidly as Rich collected records. Picking up his book, he wandered to the window.

He realized that his one vote, though not on an earthshaking matter of national importance, could have made a difference for generations to come.

Shaking his head, he began to laugh at himself. *Yeow!* he thought. *I'm starting to think like my old man.*

His attention was drawn to two young people standing at the end of the school sidewalk. Dickie and Sue Ann were engaged in conversation.

Beyond them, behind a tree in the empty lot between the school yard and the fire station, waited Harley Scott. He looked very unhappy.

Finally, Sue Ann crossed the street and began walking toward her home. Dickie turned the opposite direction, down the sidewalk toward the waiting Harley.

Dashing from the room, Rich crossed the corridor into the study hall. Opening the door, he dashed down the fire escape and across the back of the school yard.

There was going to be trouble.

It was his job to stop it.

7
An Historic Blunder

"Richard Krueger," said Mr. Hawkins, "you are the strangest student we've had in years."

"Why is that, sir?"

The principal looked at him from behind his desk. "Sit down, boy," he said. "I've been given the progress reports on your first three weeks with us.

"Your history teacher thinks you are a genius," he said, handing the anxious student the first of the slips he held in his hand. "Now, your geography teacher, on the other hand, thinks you must come from another planet."

"Another planet?"

"I didn't believe it myself, until I saw this." Mr. Hawkins handed over the map Rich had done on the continent of Africa.

"Is it that bad?"

"Unusual might be a better word. Not only did you not know most of the countries, you seem to have created places that don't even exist."

"Honest, Mr. Hawkins, I really didn't."

Rich looked at the map. "Seems fine to me."

"You're certainly inventive," said the principal. "It's bad enough you didn't know Northern Rhodesia from Southern Rhodesia, but you even changed borders."

Instantly, Rich realized what he had done.

Mr. Hawkins pointed his ruler at the map on the desk. "Zambia? Zimbabwe? Zaire? If you didn't know the answers, wouldn't it have been better to leave the spaces blank?"

Rich had taken a similar test in the spring. He had boned up for it, mastering the new names of the changing continent's many countries. In taking *this* test, he had made only one mistake.

Rich forgot it was 1944.

"Well, wouldn't it?"

"Sir?"

"Have been better to leave them blank?"

"Yes, sir, you're absolutely right about that."

Satisfied, Mr. Hawkins smiled benevolently.

"So that's the best and the worst of it. Except for your English teacher, the others think you're doing well."

"I'm happy about that." He paused. "What about Mrs. Nelson?"

"She says you are both the best reader and the worst speller she has ever seen."

Rich thought for a moment and then smiled, "All my English teachers have told me that."

Rising, Mr. Hawkins walked around the desk and patted him on the back. "All in all, though, you're making a nice adjustment to a new school."

"Thank you."

Together they walked to the door of the office.

"Odd," said the principal. "I didn't remember old man Krueger having any family."

Rich continued out of the office and down the hall to his locker. Opening it, he took out his books and headed for the stairs.

Turning the corner, he stole a quick look back toward the glass-paneled door. Framed in it, looking very mystified, stood Mr. Hawkins.

Quickly, Rich made his way down the stairs and out of the building. Maybe it was good, he reasoned, that people didn't know all that much about Mr. Krueger.

Later that evening, after supper, Rich and Mr. Krueger went into the living room. In the brief period between cleaning up the dishes and the beginning of the evening news, they found time to talk.

Though certainly capable of talking to adults, Rich never seemed to find the time, especially with his parents. Here, it was different.

Maybe it was the slower pace, or that Mr. Krueger never seemed to pry. Or because both knew the relationship was not a permanent one. Or maybe it was because he sometimes felt Mr. Krueger knew everything anyway.

"I had an interesting week at school."

"Oh?"

"The coach and some of the guys asked if I'd like to go out for the football team."

"Well, you're big enough."

"Baseball's my game," said Rich. "Besides, if I'm not to be here all that long, it's better not to get too involved."

"I think that's a wise decision." Mr. Krueger glanced at the clock and settled back in his chair.

"They're putting a lot of pressure on me, though. Especially since Tuesday."

"Something happened Tuesday?"

"Sort of. I broke up a fight at school."

"Anybody hurt?"

"Nothing serious. Dickie Branch, the kid I was talking to in front of church a couple of weeks ago, was getting picked on by Harley Scott."

"Sounds like a mismatch to me," said Mr.

Krueger. "Harley's quite a bruiser."

"If that means big and tough, you're right. Dickie and Sue Ann were talking after class one day. I guess Harley didn't like it."

"So Harley's the jealous suitor type, is he?"

"He thinks he is. The kids tell me Sue Ann doesn't like him anymore."

"That doesn't hurt your feelings, I suppose."

"Not exactly." Rich grinned.

"So you handled Harley Scott, did you?" mused Mr. Krueger. "That's quite a tall order."

"I didn't hit him. Just persuaded him it would be a good idea not to pick on guys half his size anymore."

"And he was persuaded?"

"I think he was," said Rich. "We made a deal. If he promised to leave Dickie alone, I would promise to let his face up out of the mud."

The old man laughed heartily. "I imagine Dickie was very grateful."

"Dickie didn't even see me. Harley had knocked him out with one punch."

"So you didn't hang around to receive his appreciation?"

"Naw. I'm not looking for medals. I just wish people would leave other people alone."

Mr. Krueger looked up at the tall, broad-shouldered youth and smiled.

"Underneath that manly exterior, you're a real pussycat, aren't you?"

Rich felt the redness in his face as he got up. "You talk just like Mom," he said. "It's nearly news time, and I've got homework to do."

At the door, he turned back. "Mr. Krueger?"

"Yes."

"I don't know how much longer I'll be here, and I'm not making any progress at all in finding my dad."

"I realize that, lad."

"So, I was wondering, how about giving me at least a clue?"

"No harm in that, I suppose," he said. Finding a pencil and scrap of paper, Mr. Krueger jotted a name and number on the paper and handed it to him.

"That's all you get," he said. "The rest is up to you."

In his room, Rich stared at the slip of paper. "Matthew 77?" he asked himself. "A football jersey? Probably a lineman. Backfields have lower numbers." He tried to recall who played on the line. The names swam through his head. Bob, Ken, Bill, two Jacks, but no Matt.

As it neared bedtime, Rich had ruled out the football angle as well as the possibility of it being a locker number. For whatever reason, he remembered that the school lockers were all even numbers.

He had finally eliminated his classmates altogether. There was not a Matthew in his class.

Nor could it be the class of '77; that was thirty-three years into the future.

With a sense of urgency, he set his alarm for seven the following morning. There was no time for sleeping late. He intended to be at the library door as soon as it opened.

Somehow, he was sure the answer was there.

8
Following the Clue

Sharply at eight, the librarian opened the door. By 8:03, Rich had settled himself in the reference section. It was nearing ten o'clock when he closed the town registry. Rubbing his eyes, he wondered where to look next.

"The answer has to be here somewhere," he said softly.

"It usually is," answered a voice. "Can I be of help?"

Rich turned to see the librarian standing behind him. "I hope so," he said. "I've been looking everywhere I can think of for someone who lives or used to live here."

The librarian sat down across from him. "Is this someone in particular?"

Rich hesitated. He remembered Mr. Krueger's admonition: Don't complicate things that can't be complicated.

Rich decided his question was worth the risk. "Is there a Richard Lawler living here in Baxterville?"

The words rang strangely in his ears, as though he were asking about himself. He had never seen the librarian before and counted on her not knowing him.

"Richard Lawler?" It was obvious the name meant nothing to her. "It's not in the directory?"

"No, ma'am."

She searched her memory "Lowery . . . Lawson . . . Langley . . . no, they moved away last year. Is that L-A-W-L-E-R?"

"That's right."

"It's a small town, but the name doesn't ring a bell," she replied. "Could he live out in the countryside?"

"I'm not sure."

"Might be a tenant farmer out Baldon Road somewhere."

"Who else could I check with?" asked Rich.

"Try Mr. Dolan over at the post office. He knows more people than I do."

"I'll give it a try. Thanks."

"Is there somewhere I can reach you if I come up with anything?"

"I don't think so," Rich said. "I'm sort of only passing through."

Leaving the library, he walked down two blocks and crossed over to the big stone post office. When the lobby was clear, he approached the man at the window.

"Is the postmaster in?"

"Not on Saturdays, son," said the man. "Can I help?"

"The lady at the library sent me over," Rich explained. "I'm looking for a family named Lawler. Richard Lawler. She thought the post-master might be able to help."

The man behind the counter looked thought-ful. "I'm the rural carrier Monday through Friday. Far as I know, there's no one on my route by that name."

"You're sure?"

"Positive."

"Okay. Thanks anyway."

Rich headed for the door.

"Wait a minute, son," said the man.

"Yes?" answered Rich. "You thought of someone?"

" 'Fraid not," he said. "A piece of paper fell out of your pocket."

Rich picked it up. It was the note Mr. Krueger had given him the night before. Looking at it carefully, he returned to the window.

"Excuse me again, but do you happen to have a Matthew or Matthews family on your route?"

The man behind the window searched his memory. "Nope," he said. "Did have a Matthews once, couple years back. Husband went in the service; the wife went back to her folks."

"Oh, well, it was just a long shot."

"Wait a minute, now," added the man behind the window. "There's a Matthew Johnson just moved in as a tenant farmer. Would that be any help?"

"Could be," Rich said. "What's his address?"

"They don't have addresses out there, boy. Only mailbox numbers."

Rich looked again at the slip of paper. "Is it possible their number is seventy-seven?"

"Seventy-seven. As a matter of fact, it is." The man looked startled. "How could you possibly know that?"

"That must be the place," Rich said excitedly. "How do I get there?"

"Know where Baker's Corners is? About two miles out of town?"

Rich nodded.

"Turn right on the gravel road. It'll be the second mailbox on the right."

Stuffing the note back into his pocket, Rich dashed for the door. "Thanks, Mister," he yelled.

Dashing down the steps, he headed up Main Street toward home, trying to imagine what connection there might be between a new tenant farmer and his missing father.

While Mr. Krueger might have been a lot more helpful, Rich was convinced Mr. Krueger would not deliberately send him on a wild-goose chase.

By the time he reached the top of the hill, his breath was coming in giant gasps. At the sidewalk to the porch, he slowed down and walked inside.

Mr. Krueger was not around. Rich was glad. He didn't want to see the man until he could confront him with his solution.

He took the pitcher of lemonade from the refrigerator, poured himself a glass and drank it down. The ice-cold drink sent a pain through the roof of his mouth, but he was too excited to notice.

When he went to the garage for his bike, he saw Mr. Krueger in the backyard. Unable to resist the temptation, Rich called out, "Thanks for the clue, Grandpa!"

He jumped on the bike and headed down the hill. Two blocks past the post office, he stopped for the town's only traffic light before making the left turn that would take him out to Baker's Corners.

As he pedaled along the dusty country road,

the muscles in the calves of his legs began to bunch up. Slowing a bit, he began to push down with his heels, easing the ache.

Finally, he reached an intersection and turned right onto the gravel lane. There were no mailboxes in sight. A half mile farther on, he passed the first one. In the distance, he could see the second sitting in front of a brown shingled house. He pedaled faster, nearly sliding sideways on the road's loose gravel.

As he neared the Johnson place, Rich wondered what to say when he got there. He checked the mailbox, freshly painted with the name and box number: M. Johnson 77

He turned into the driveway and parked the bike. Crossing the lawn, he approached the small wooden porch. As he knocked on the door, Rich wondered if he were nearing the end of his search.

9
Tragedy in Baxterville

Rich sat dejectedly on the steps of the front porch, staring across Elm to the empty lot. His crazy trip back into time was leaving him more frustrated each day. The one bright spot in his three-week adventure was the discovery that his mother was as great a person in her youth as he could have hoped for. At times, the urge to go up to her in class and tell her so was almost overwhelming.

The search for his father had turned into a series of dead ends. His long bike trip out into the country the weekend before had come to nothing, serving only to leave the farmer and his wife thoroughly confused by the purpose of his visit.

Further, he was beginning to resent Mr. Krueger's determined reluctance to make his search easier. He heard the front door open behind him.

"Time you should be leaving for school, young man."

"Yes, sir," said Rich. "I guess I got carried away with my troubles."

"Didn't know you had any," Mr. Krueger commented. "How are things going at school?"

"Okay, I guess." He forced a grin. "I'm even beginning to take an interest in history."

"Making any friends?"

"That's part of the problem. Since I know I won't be around here forever, I'm sort of wandering around the edges of everything."

"How about Harley?"

"We talk in the halls. Mom—Sue Ann hangs around Dickie like a clucking hen. I guess it's the mother instinct in her. As for the rest of the kids, they're all right."

"Sounds to me as though you're beginning to miss your friends."

Rich thought of Julie and his parents.

"You're probably right," he said. Getting up from the steps, Rich grabbed his books. "But no matter what happens, I'm going to find my old—

my dad before I have to go back."

"That's the spirit!" said Mr. Krueger. "Three cheers for you."

Rich headed down the sidewalk. Halfway to the street, he turned back toward Mr. Krueger. "I have a feeling time is running out. I'll be a little late tonight. There is one more hot lead I have to pursue."

"Good luck," Mr. Krueger called out. "You'll be home for supper, won't you?"

"What are we having?"

"If I tell you, you won't show up. It's nearly the end of the month. You've eaten me out of ration stamps."

Walking down the hill, Rich wished Mr. Krueger hadn't mentioned rationing. He felt guilty sharing what little the old man was allowed each month. Sometimes when he thought about Harley, he got very angry about those who didn't do their share.

His stomach, unfilled by his breakfast bowl of cereal and milk, rumbled ominously as he walked. Rich wished it would stop. He realized being patriotic was more than cheering at a John Wayne movie.

Rich entered the school yard just as first bell sounded, leaving him five minutes to reach his first class. He wished the school day was over so he could follow his latest lead.

Steve had given him the idea. He told Rich

about a one-room school four miles west of town where his uncle taught. The district had planned on closing it in 1942. Instead, it had decided to keep the school open for the duration of the war.

Rich planned to go out there after school and talk with Steve's uncle. Maybe this time his search would have a happier ending.

His jaunty attitude lasted until he entered the building. As he climbed the stairs to his first class, he felt a somberness in the air about him. The other students entering the classroom were talking in hushed voices. Rich tried to hear what was being said.

Mr. Wilson, the science teacher, was already at his desk. When the bell rang, he addressed the class. "Some of you may have heard the terrible news," he said. "Oliver Branch, the father of one of our students, was killed in an auto accident late last night."

A gasp came from the class. "How did it happen?" someone asked.

"As best the police can tell, he was run off the road by a speeding car."

Stunned, Rich looked around the room. The desk where Dickie sat was empty, of course. His eyes traveled slowly toward the window. The last desk by the window was vacant. That was where Harley Scott normally sat.

"Open your books to page forty-three," said Mr. Wilson "Will someone please explain convection for us?"

The class was still.

Finally, Rich raised his hand. "It's the transmission of heat or electricity by the mass movement of particles," he said.

"Correct," said the teacher. "Now who can tell us . . . ?"

Rich's mind wandered from the movement of particles to his own movement from time present to time past. Mr. Branch, whom he'd never met, had moved from life to death. Rich thought of the vast world of knowledge and how little of it he understood.

He wondered where all the answers were. . . .

"One more thing before the bell rings," Mr. Wilson said. "The junior class picture will be taken tomorrow after lunch period, down in the gym."

It was halfway through Latin class that the significance of the announcement came to him.

At last it was lunchtime. Rich dashed for the door and headed home as fast as he could. "Be there, Grandpa, be there," he gasped as he ran.

Reaching the top of the hill, Rich cut across the yard and dashed up the steps of the porch. Once inside, he paused to catch his breath.

"Grandpa? Are you home?"

He went into the kitchen and saw the old man climbing the back steps. Mr. Krueger carried a load of wood. Rich opened the door and helped unload the wood.

"I'm glad you chopped and split this for me," said Mr. Krueger. "It would have been quite a job for an old coot like me."

"Winter will be here sooner than you know," Rich said. "This wood might cut down on your coal bill."

"It was very thoughtful of you. You could have been off playing Saturday."

"Yeah," said Rich. "Or joyriding with Harley Scott."

Inside, they sat down at the kitchen table.

"What brings you home at lunchtime?"

Rich paused for a moment before he answered. "I'm afraid my visit here is almost over."

"Oh. What makes you think that?"

"It's been a hectic day at school. Our class picture will be taken tomorrow."

"And it's obvious you can't be seen in that."

"I wish I'd voted to ban the yearbook, then Mrs. Nelson would have done the same."

"But that would have changed the future," Mr. Krueger reminded him. "You couldn't do that. Every action we take affects other people, and they, in turn, affect many others."

"Finding Sue Ann—my mother—didn't do that, did it?"

"Not at all. Nothing you did has changed her life in any way. As you put it yourself, you've been mostly an observer."

Rich thought before speaking. "I know I only have about twenty-four hours left to observe. I'll be gone from this time before that picture is taken tomorrow, won't I?"

"I'm afraid so," Mr. Krueger said gravely.

"There is so much left to do. I was going out to the country schoolhouse this afternoon to see if my dad is enrolled out there. And this terrible thing with Dickie's father. . . ."

"I heard about it," said Mr. Krueger. "Tragic. I suppose the boy isn't in school today."

"No, and neither is Harley Scott. Do you think there could be some connection?"

"Hard to tell."

"I should go out to the Branches' this afternoon. They're new in town, just like me. Maybe there is something I could do."

"That's a very Christian attitude," said Mr. Krueger.

"But there's so little time. I can't do both. The school and the Branches' place are both way out in the country, on opposite sides of town. It would be impossible."

"What do you think you should do?"

"Could you possibly drive me?" he asked anxiously.

Mr. Krueger sighed deeply, "I wish I could, my boy. Unfortunately, my gas coupons are gone, and the tank is nearly dry."

"Rationing!" said Rich bitterly. "I'm sick of hearing that word. We can buy whatever we want, whenever we want it."

"You live in a blessed time. You should be anxious to get back to it."

"So it's one or the other, Grandpa. What do I do, continue the search or visit Dickie?"

"That's a question only you can answer, I'm afraid," said Mr. Krueger. "So far you've done pretty well."

Rich was not yet ready to give up.

"How about just one more clue? I promise I won't ask for any more."

Mr. Krueger reached behind him, taking the last apple from the bowl on the counter. "Eat this on your way back to school. I can hear your stomach protesting."

"Grandpa!" said Rich dejectedly, reaching for the apple. "Just *one* little clue."

"All right," said the old man. "I'll give you one that you'll receive and give many times over during your life."

Hungrily, Rich took a bite from the apple. "What is it, Grandpa? Tell me."

"Remember the Golden Rule."

"That's all you'll tell me?"

"That's *almost* all you need."

"Thanks, I guess," said Rich. "I'll think about that on the way back to class."

Nearing the school yard, he was still mysti-

fied. Shaking his head, he mumbled to himself,
"Doggone him, anyway. He sure doesn't make
things easy for a person."

10
When Puzzles Don't Fit

The Golden Rule sounded vaguely familiar. Curious, Rich decided to look it up during his study hall.

After rushing through his math homework, he asked for a library pass and headed down the hall. Since his Saturday morning at the public library, he felt like an expert on reference books.

Bartlett's Familiar Quotations was hardly unknown to him. He'd used it often, helping to catch his father up in an error.

"Golden Rule" referred him to a page near the front of the book. Finding it, he read: "Therefore, all things whatsoever ye would that men should do to you, do ye even so to them."

Rich pondered the phrase and its modern version: "Do unto others as you would have them do unto you."

He wished Mr. Krueger didn't always make things so difficult. How, he wondered, would this help him comfort Dickie?

Puzzled, he put the large book back on the shelf and returned to the study hall. For the balance of the period, he stared out the window at the turning leaves.

When the wind came up, a few leaves fluttered downward. Rich wondered why the most colorful ones always fell first.

Slowly, an idea came to him. Both he and Dickie, each in his own way, had suffered a loss. Dickie's was sudden and tragic, happening here and now. Rich's was more a lack of discovery than a loss; he knew his father was there in the future world to which he'd return.

He felt a little selfish for putting his own problem first. During his last class, he decided to postpone his new lead and go to Dickie's house instead.

When the last bell had rung, he called Mr. Krueger from the pay phone in the hall. "Decided the Branches have more problems than I do. Thought I'd go over there before coming home."

"A very nice idea. What about the investigation you were going to conduct?"

"It'll have to wait, I guess."

"You may not have much more time."

"I know, but if I were in Dickie's shoes, I might like someone to talk to."

"That philosophy sounds familiar," said Mr. Krueger.

"Yeah," said Rich. "I think it's called the Golden Rule."

The old man chuckled. "All right, then. I'll expect you home for supper."

"I'll be there. Grandpa? You're pretty crafty, you know that?"

"More so than you think," said Mr. Krueger. "See you later."

Hanging up the phone, Rich gathered his books. "Why does he do that to me?" he mumbled. "Now he's got me curious again."

"Thank you for coming, Rich," said Mrs. Branch. "This is a very sad day for us. I'll tell Dickie you're here. He'll be glad to see you."

"I'll wait out back," Rich mumbled, gesturing vaguely with his hand. Not knowing what to do or say, he wandered around the side of the house.

In the backyard, he saw an old apple tree heavy with fruit. He picked the reddest apple he could find and polished it on his corduroy pants.

As he chewed on the apple, Rich wondered if

he had done the right thing. He'd never been to a funeral or been around when anyone died. When he'd lost his grandmother, back in the East, his folks went, leaving him with friends.

Rich gazed out at the railroad tracks that cut their endless path through the countryside beyond. From far off in the distance came the deep whistle of a train. Soon, on the horizon, he saw a trail of smoke as it drew closer.

"Wouldn't it be something," he said softly to the wind, "if my dad was coming into town on that train. And me sitting out here in the country, I'd miss him completely."

Rich knew he was thinking crazy again. The frustrating search for his father was beginning to drive him looney.

Thump!

He felt something carom off his head, followed by a high-pitched laugh. When he turned around, Dickie was standing behind him.

How can he be laughing? Rich wondered.

"Who are you, Isaac Newton?" Dickie asked.

"Isaac who?"

"Isaac Newton. The law of gravity has already been discovered, you know."

"Huh?"

"The apple that hit you on the head. According to legend, that's what started Newton thinking about the effects of gravity. We learned that in General Science last year."

"Maybe *you* did," said Rich, rubbing his head. "I don't think *I* did."

They sat watching the approaching train. At the nearby crossing, its whistle sounded again as an endless row of freight cars raced by.

"Hoped it might be a passenger train," said Rich.

"You expecting someone?"

"In a way, I suppose."

Finally the caboose passed and disappeared in the distance.

"Rich?"

"Yeah?"

"Thanks for coming over."

Rich dropped his head and stared at the ground. "Yeah. I figured I ought to."

"I appreciate it. Now there's just Ma and me again."

"Must be tough to take."

"At least he's with God. Mom says that will make it easier."

"You really believe that?"

"I really do. Miss him already. Probably feel worse when the shock wears off."

"Never been through it myself," said Rich.

"Mom says we can't really feel sorry for him. He has eternal life in a far better world than this."

"Suppose you're right. It's you and your mom suffering the real loss."

Thump.

Another apple dropped from the tree, hitting Dickie squarely on the head. Caught by surprise, Rich threw back his head and laughed. "Sorry," he apologized, "I couldn't help it."

"We were getting too serious, anyway," said Dickie. "What do you suppose the odds are of that happening to each of us in the same day?"

"Don't ask me, wise guy," said Rich. "You're the math genius, not me."

"Maybe I'll get a bushel basket and pick the rest later. Want to take a few home?"

"No, I . . ." Rich hesitated. "Well, maybe a couple."

The boys walked back to Rich's bike. He put the apples in the carrier.

"I'll get the basket," said Dickie. "It'll keep me busy till supper."

"And I'd better get home."

They looked at each other awkwardly.

Dickie put out his hand. "Thanks again for coming out."

Rich returned the shake. "I'm glad I did," he said. He walked his bike up the short lane to the road, got on, and started back toward town.

Most of the way, he thought of Dickie. Then his thoughts turned to the book of quotations. When he was five blocks from home, it hit him. The page in the book popped back into focus. As he turned the corner, the pieces of the puzzle seemed to fall into place.

It was all as clear as could be. He had scanned right over it. Pulling into the driveway, Rich jumped off his bike. Like a shot, he was across the lawn and into the house.

"Where's the fire?" Mr. Krueger asked.

"I think I'm on to something."

"Good for you."

In the living room, Rich removed a book from the shelf. Finding what he was searching for, he read it quickly, stopped, and read it again.

Slamming the book shut, he returned it to the shelf and walked disconsolately to the kitchen. He sat at the table, slumping in his chair.

"You didn't find what you were looking for?"

"I found it all right," said Rich. "When I looked up the Golden Rule in school, I ran my finger down the page in a hurry. On the way home, I saw that page again in my mind's eye. The quotation was from the Bible, Matthew seven, verse twelve.

Mr. Krueger continued peeling potatoes.

"And?"

"And then it dawned on me. When you wrote Matthew on that piece of paper, you meant the *book* of Matthew.

"And the number wasn't seventy-seven. It was chapter seven, verse seven."

The old man put the last potato into a bowl of water. He nodded appreciatively. "You're a good detective, my boy."

"But I still don't get it," Rich said. "All it says is, 'Ask, and it shall be given you; seek, and ye shall find; knock, and it shall be opened unto you.'"

"Exactly."

"Exactly!" said Rich, sharply. "Exactly? Why are you playing these games with me?"

"You look quite annoyed," said Mr. Krueger.

"Why shouldn't I be? You've had me chasing all over town!"

Pulling the bicycle clip from his pants leg, Rich threw it across the kitchen floor.

"Ask, and it shall be given you!" He stood up angrily and pushed back the chair. "I've been asking all over town. The librarian, the guy in the post office, the police, everyone I could think of. What kind of clue was that?"

"Some things in life you can't do by yourself. And there are other things no one else can do for you either."

"So then what?" Rich asked. "Who's left to ask?"

"Try God," said Mr. Krueger. "Try God."

11
A Race Against Time

When Rich awoke the following morning, he knew that for him it was the last day of 1944.

Brushing his teeth, he debated whether it was worth going to school or not. According to the clock, he only had six hours left till the picture-taking session.

Rich had almost made up his mind to skip school when it dawned on him: maybe this was the day his father's family moved to town. Convinced he would find his answer, Rich finished dressing and went downstairs for breakfast.

Mr. Krueger was standing over the stove as he entered the kitchen.

"Grandpa," Rich said hesitantly, "I'm sorry I lost my temper last night and stormed out of the room."

"Understandable, my boy. Playing by the rules set down for us isn't always easy." Mr. Krueger turned his attention from the sizzling pan. His eyes were damp. "I've enjoyed your visit here. I'll be sorry to see you go."

Rich put his arm around the old man's shoulders. "I wish I could take you with me."

"That's a nice thought," said Mr. Krueger. He slid the contents of the pan onto a plate. "I fixed you a special treat for this morning's breakfast. Two eggs and bacon."

Rich looked at the plate. "But those are the last two eggs we had. You shouldn't have."

"Nonsense. October will be here in no time, and I'll have a new ration book."

Rich ate the meal hastily, with both relish and guilt. He washed off the plate, dried it, and returned it to the cupboard.

"Don't forget," said Mr. Krueger.

"I know," Rich answered. "They're taking the picture at 1:30. I'll be back before then."

Halfway down the hill, he passed the Community Church. On impulse, he climbed the steps and went inside. There was a simple austerity to the narthex. It didn't appear greatly different from the last time he'd seen it. As he walked up the aisle, Rich recalled the great comfort he used to find as a child in God's house.

He thought of kindly Mr. Krueger, whom he would probably never see again. He thought of the students of his parents' generation. They grew up in a time when one could be caring, patriotic, and devoted to God without being ridiculed by many of one's peers.

Mr. Krueger's words came back to him: Try God.

Before falling asleep the previous night, Rich had read the seventh chapter of Matthew over and over. From it had come the encouragement to pray.

"Judge not, that ye be not judged." Remembering that, his ill feelings toward Harley Scott began to disappear. That, too, he'd read in Matthew. Perhaps, as Mr. Krueger said, when Harley's burdens become too heavy to bear, he will turn to the Lord. Rich prayed that he would.

"Dear God," he said softly, "for whatever purpose you've brought me here, let me do the work you've intended for me. Help me understand, Lord. I know now there is nowhere else to turn."

Rich left the church feeling more at peace than he had in a long time. He went on to school knowing it would be for just half a day.

Noon came, and Rich left his books in his locker. At the end of the hall, a group of students gossiped excitedly.

"Did you hear the latest?" Steve Kristl asked.

"The latest?" said Rich. "What's happened?"

"About Harley? It was Harley's car!"

"What about it?"

"He was the one who ran Mr. Branch off the road." Steve paused for breath. "They found a dent and matching paint."

"That's terrible," said Rich. "How can he possibly face Dickie after this?"

"I'm glad I'm not in Harley's shoes."

Rich knew why Dickie was not in school. He'd been so involved in his own departure, he'd failed to realize that Harley was missing today, too.

Had his prayer for Harley come too late? He wished he could see Dickie one more time.

It seemed unfair he must leave in less than two hours. This was a time when a person really needed a friend.

Returning to his locker, Rich started to open it and take out his lunch.

And then he changed his mind.

Dashing out of the school, he pulled his bike from the rack. Where should he go? Harley's or Dickie's?

Pedaling as hard as he could, Rich passed the village limit sign and turned onto the country road. Twenty minutes later he braked to a stop in front of a small white porch.

The front door opened. "I was afraid I wouldn't see you again," said Dickie Branch.

"This is a terrible time to intrude. I needed someone to talk to."

"How about a glass of milk?" Dickie asked. "You look all sweaty."

"Thanks," said Rich, "but I haven't much time. Can we just sit and talk?"

"Sure. Mother's in town at the funeral parlor."

Rich was having doubts about having come, but he went on. "I need someone to talk to before I leave. Mr. Krueger puts too many restrictions on what I can say."

"I know how you feel," said Dickie. "I've been living under some restrictions of my own."

"You have?" asked Rich. He wanted to get on with his story—to tell someone of the adventure he'd been on, of the triumphs and frustrations of his half successful search. The impatience must have shown on his face.

"I'm sorry," said Dickie. "You had something you wanted to say."

Reluctantly, Rich pushed aside his feelings. "It can wait a few minutes. Go on with whatever you were going to tell me."

"It makes me feel good that you're willing to confide in me." Dickie turned to watch a car passing on the highway. "I thought maybe I'd let something slip yesterday when I said that Mother and I were alone again."

"Again?" Rich asked. "Was that what I missed?"

"Uh huh." Dickie hesitated. "You see, my mother was married once before."

"And divorced?"

Dickie shook his head. "That's what makes it so rough on her. Two husbands killed in less than three years."

"Wow," said Rich.

"My real father died during the attack on Pearl Harbor. Maybe that's why I don't share Harley's enthusiasm for war movies."

Things were starting to fall in place in Rich's mind.

"People like Harley can't separate fact from fiction," Rich said. "Everything is black or white to them, with no shades of gray." He sighed. "Maybe he'll change."

It was evident to Rich that Dickie did not yet know of Harley's apparent involvement in his stepfather's death. Rich decided there was no point in mentioning it.

"It got worse after Mr. Branch met Mom," Dickie continued. "And worse still just before we moved here."

"You didn't want your mother to marry again?"

116

"I didn't mind that so much." Dickie kicked absently at the porch railing. "He was a nice enough man, all right. Always anxious to put the best front on things, though."

"Nothing wrong with that, I suppose."

"When we moved here to Baxterville, he thought it would look better if we appeared to be just a normal family."

"I don't understand. Weren't you?"

"He felt funny about being a stepfather. Didn't want people asking questions and prying into Mom's business. I suppose he did what he thought was right."

"I guess it worked," said Rich. "Nobody's prying into your life. Who would object to whatever he did?"

A look of defiance flashed in Dickie's eyes. The young man stood up and walked into the yard. "I would," he said. As he turned, Rich saw his eyes filled with tears. "I'm proud of my real father."

"You had every right to be," agreed Rich. "He died defending his country."

"Then you think I'm right in wanting to use my real name?"

"Of course," said Rich. "What is your real name?"

Proudly, Dickie straightened up. "It will be good to say it to someone again. My name is Richard Alan Lawler, Jr."

Rich sat stunned.

Maybe it had all been planned this way, that he get to know and respect his father before discovering who he was. He thought back to his brief stop in the church that morning. *Surely,* he said to himself, *God works in a mysterious way.*

"Well?" said Dickie.

"Richard Alan Lawler. That sounds like a pretty good name to me."

"I think so, too," said Dickie. "I nearly forgot. You had something you wanted to tell me."

Rich glanced at his watch. "Actually, it wasn't all that important," he said. "Anyway, it's later than I realized. I've got to be on my way."

Dickie walked over, put his hand on the taller boy's shoulder, and shook his hand. "Thanks for coming out," he said. "You're the only visitors we've had except for Sue Ann and her parents last night."

"A real nice girl, that Sue Ann," Rich commented. "She'd make a real great girl friend for you."

"I should be so lucky," Dickie smiled.

"You'd *better* be so lucky," said Rich. He got on his bike and headed out toward the road.

"Let's talk again sometime," called Dickie.

"I'd like that," Rich said. "In fact, I'll guarantee it."

12
The Last Puzzle Piece

It was nearly one o'clock when Rich set off for town. Ten minutes later, at the village limits, he slowed the bike, but his mind kept racing to take in the events of the past hour.

After discovering the true identity of his newly found, and soon to be lost, friend, Rich marveled over the transformation from boy to man. Dickie, his dad, must have grown rapidly in his late teens, and his squeaky voice deepened with the growth.

Years of Mom's good cooking had amply filled out his skinny frame, but through all the changes

Rich could see the similarities in boy and man.

He had come to like the quiet Dickie. Now it was over, although Rich realized he would see him for years to come. But the relationship would be father and son, not classmate to classmate. The two could never be the same.

Still, he vowed to make his family a more important part of his life, the way it had been when he was younger.

Turning onto Main, Rich stood up on the pedals, pushing the bike hard up the long hill toward Ninth Street.

The overhanging clock at the bank said 1:15.

Halfway between Fourth and Fifth, Rich gave in to the laws of gravity and walked the two-wheeler the rest of the way.

He stored the bike in the back of the garage and crossed the lawn to the house.

"Grandpa!" he called out, opening the front door. "Grandpa, where are you?"

There was only silence.

Rich climbed the stairs quickly. At the landing he called again, "Grandpa, wait till I tell you what happened today."

Still no one answered.

Entering his bedroom, Rich checked his clock. One twenty.

He looked out the window toward the vacant lot, then up and down the street.

"Come home, Grandpa," he called. "I've got

to say good-bye one more time."

His feet were sore from wearing thin, wartime sneakers. Reaching down, he removed them and lay back on the bed to wait.

In a little while, Rich realized he was wasting precious time. Getting up from the bed, he ran down the stairs and out onto the porch.

The family car pulled into the driveway, its roof nearly touching the lowest branch of the massive oak.

Rich bounced down off the porch.

"You're back," he hollered. "And so am I!"

"Of course, dear," said his mother. "Dad and I only went to the early movie after dinner."

"Only a dollar seventy-five if you catch the first show," said his father. "Can't afford the four bucks apiece you youngsters spend."

Rich smiled tolerantly as the middle-aged couple approached. He looked closely at his mother. The beauty of the young Sue Ann was still there, radiating from her eyes.

"Whatcha been up to?" smiled his dad. "You look kind of bleary-eyed."

"I lay down for a while," said Rich. "Spent some time reminiscing about the good old days."

His father grinned. "When was that? When you were twelve?"

Rich opened the door for his parents, and they walked into the front hall.

"No, I mean back in the forties. When you were a boy."

"I don't believe it," said his mother.

"Back when you and Mom first met."

"We haven't looked at the high school pictures in years," his dad said. "You really interested in that old stuff?"

"Sure," said Rich. "It might be fun. Where's your old yearbook?"

"It's in the cabinet under the bookshelves somewhere," his mother answered.

"Come on, dear. I'll help you look," his dad added eagerly.

His mother hesitated. "Are you hungry, Rich? Should I fix you a snack first?"

"Why don't you help Dad? Let me be the host this time."

"Can I believe what I'm hearing?" said his puzzled father.

"Shush, dear," Mother said.

Later, with the photo albums stacked on the floor, Dick Lawler pushed back the last of the soft drink on his tray. "That was quite a spread you fixed," he told Rich.

"Your scrambled eggs with catsup were really delicious," his mother added.

"Like Italian-style eggplant," his father said, "without the plant."

"I'll clean up, son, since I didn't have to prepare the snack." His mother began stacking their empty plates.

As she reached the kitchen, the telephone rang. "It's for you, Rich. I think it's Julie."

Rich closed a scrapbook and set it aside. "Please tell her I'll call back later." His eyes fell on the 1944 yearbook. "Thanks," he said, as his mother returned.

He opened the yearbook. "That's not the year you two graduated, was it?"

"We were the class of '45," said his dad. "Did I ever tell you the story of how we gave up our yearbook for the paper drive?" He hesitated, then began to laugh. "About a hundred times, I imagine."

Rich grinned. "One hundred and twelve, to be exact."

His parents looked over his shoulder as Rich turned the pages.

"Oh, dear," said his mother. "I looked so awful then."

"Come on, I'll bet you were the prettiest girl in the class."

"She certainly was," his dad answered. "I don't know what she saw in me."

Rich thought back to his last glimpse of Dickie. *And neither do I.*

He turned one more page.

"There I am," his mother said. "Look at that long hair!"

A strange feeling came over Rich as the

smiling faces he had been with earlier in the day peered back at him from the yellowing pages. Then he asked the question he knew he must ask; the one to which he already knew the answer. "Where's the picture of you, Dad?"

"There was a death in the family that week. My picture never got taken."

"Too bad," said Rich. "I'll bet you were the handsomest, strongest guy in the class."

Blushing a bit, his father turned to his wife and winked. "Why, of course I was. What would you expect?"

"I don't know," teased Rich. "Someone quiet and skinny, maybe."

"Shame on you, Richard Lawler. Your father was always the handsomest man I ever met." Reaching over, Mother took her husband's hand.

Rich saw the notation at the bottom of the page.

"It says here that you and a Harley Scott were absent." He thought of the young man he'd included in his prayers that morning in church.

"A strange story, that," his father responded. "The day the pictures were taken, the police were questioning him."

"What did he do?"

"They thought he killed someone with his car. The following day it came out that he was protecting his father who actually had been driving the car."

"What happened to him after that?"

"A complete transformation," said his mother. "Harley went on to college and ended up in the Korean War."

"Was he killed?" Rich wondered if real life had dimmed the young Harley's love of wartime movies.

"No," said his dad. "In fact, he came out of the war as a genuine hero. He saved the lives of three men under fire."

"Even though he didn't go in the service to be a fighting man," his mother added.

Rich wondered at that. Maybe Harley ended up as an ambulance-driving conscientious objector.

"After the war," his father continued, "his profession took him from place to place. Finally it brought him back here to Baxterville."

"Here?" asked Rich. "He's living here?"

"You're taking quite an interest in someone you've never seen, aren't you?"

"The missing picture makes him kind of mysterious, I guess," said Rich. "Have I ever seen him?"

"Probably not." His father chuckled. "You don't hang out in his kind of place."

"Dad, I got to admit. You've told me a story I've never heard before."

At the end of the evening, Rich said, "I

enjoyed this. Let's do it again."

"We're always here," his father replied.

Later, when he was upstairs in his room, Rich thought of the adventure he'd had. He would miss the quieter pace of his parents' youth, their unquestioning love of God and country, and the values that everyone seemed to accept.

Yet he missed the conveniences when he was away: the television and stereo, the more casual dress in the schools, the feeling of money in his pocket, and the abundance of items to buy.

But most of all, he would miss Mr. Krueger. Somehow, the old man had managed to direct his thinking without ever actually telling him what to do.

And he thought of his renewed faith in God. He was glad he had gone, but he was glad to be back.

Suddenly, he remembered his promise to Mr. Krueger. Leaping up from the bed, he dashed down the stairs. Seated in the living room, his parents looked up as he entered.

"By the way," Rich said hesitantly, "I've set my alarm. If you'd like, I'll come along to church with you in the morning."

His parents exchanged glances.

"We'd be glad to have you," said his mother.

"See you in the morning, son," added his father.

The following morning, the three of them

attended the service. Rich saw, much to his surprise, that many of his friends were in the congregation. He listened to the sermon closely. The minister's words intrigued him.

The closing hymn was one he knew well. It was one of Mr. Krueger's favorites. Somehow, in this house of God, he realized there were some truths the passing of time would never change.

When the service ended, they walked down the aisle, toward the minister who stood greeting the departing members. Reaching him, Mr. Lawler paused. "Pastor, I'd like you to meet our boy."

Extending his hand, Rich smiled at the gray-haired, distinguished-looking man.

"Son," said his father, "I'd like you to meet the Reverend Harley Scott."